On the Other Side

Written by Myth and Magic Crew 10

Aafreen Jessani
Charlotte Hansen
Marcus Lau
Mischa Wijesekera
Saffron Gibson
Siena Chiaradia
Sophia Alfano
Veronica Pare

Under the direction of Emily Rodriguez and Written Out Loud Studios

Cover design by Naomi Giddings

On the Other Side© 2021 by the members of Myth and Magic Crew 10. All rights reserved under the Pan-American and International Copyright Conventions. This book may not be reproduced in whole or in part, except for brief quotations embodied in critical articles or reviews, in any form or by any means, electronic or mechanical, including photocopying, recording, or by any information storage and retrieval system now known or hereinafter invented, without written permission of the authors and/or Written Out Loud Studios.

ISBN 978-1-312-67921-4

This book is dedicated to all the loving parents and supporters of this crew, and to each other.

To Mr. Hewson,
Thank you for your continued support and guidance. I hope you enjoy this book that I have co-authored (see if you can find my writing :)).

Sincerely,

Marcus Lau

Contents

Prologue 1
Chapter 1 - I Bid Farewell to a Bunch of Buildings 5
Chapter 2 - I Get My Powers, Sort Of 9
Chapter 3 - I Get Taken to Prison 19
Chapter 4 - A Lady Says a Lot of Words 29
Chapter 5 - I Meet Fireboy and Watergirl 41
Chapter 6 - Maybe This Quest is A Bad Idea 49
Chapter 7 - Open Sesame 53
Chapter 8 - We Wake Up an Ancient Death Machine 69
Chapter 9 - We Nearly Become Supper 73
Chapter 10 - I Hate Tests 85
Chapter 11 - We Don't Put it Back and I Dodge a Question 91
Chapter 12 - Tea Time With the Wizard Who Speaks Nonsense 95
Chapter 13 - I Am Told to Leave 101
Chapter 14 - I Climb an Endless Staircase 105
Chapter 15 - The Microwave Returns 111
Chapter 16 - There's Nothing in My Bag, I Promise 119
Chapter 17 - Fighting a Crystal Dragon is Very Hard 125

Chapter 18 - I Have a Love Life? 129
Chapter 19 - Your Hamster is Very Slow 137
Chapter 20 - The Prisoner is Back 143
Chapter 21 - Where is the Fifth Stone? 149
Chapter 22 - Walking Through Ruins 155
Chapter 23 - Arrest or Kill? 159
Chapter 24 - I Go on a Killing Spree 165
Chapter 25 - I Lose It 173
Chapter 26 - I Blow Up a City 179
Chapter 27 - I Relive the Worst Moment of My Life 187
Chapter 28 - I Struggle to Make a Choice 199
Chapter 29 - Origin Stories Are Always Tragic 211
Chapter 30 - I Count Bricks... 221
Chapter 31 - The Council Decides My Fate...................... 225
Chapter 32 - I Leave, Goodbye! 229
Chapter 33 - My Turn 239
Epilogue... 245
About the Authors 249

Prologue

It's quite hard to start a council meeting with a missing member.

"Where is she?" Councillor Marina muttered, staring at the door, half-expecting councillor Gaia to walk in at that very moment.

"She's late again, no surprise," Councillor Zephyr grumbled.

"We've got to start to start without her. We have more pressing matters at hand than the fact that Gaia can't manage her time properly," Councillor Vulcan reminded them.

"With Scribe Dodona repairing damage in sector four, we have three members. That's not good enough, but I suppose we can start," Zephyr said.

Everyone went silent.

"I believe we all know why we're here," Councillor Marina finally said.

Her fellow council members simply stared elsewhere, doing anything to avoid this conversation. No one needed to hear this right now.

"There's no law that says this witch has to live," Councillor Zephyr offered.

"I believe it's better to avoid death altogether. We could simply lock them up instead," Councillor Marina said.

Zephyr rolled his eyes, and made an effort to make sure Marina saw it. "No one needs your compassion right now. People are being killed."

"The prophecy was already fulfilled. I don't understand. That man. The one in Magi prison. He was the one. I thought this was done! His reign of terror still sends shivers down people's spines. He had to be the one. So why is this happening again? The sectors can't survive another attack such as this! But this person is only sixteen. I don't believe death is the best idea," Marina said sharply.

"They're a danger. I believe death is the best option at the moment," Vulcan put in.

"No!"

"Shut it."

The council dipped into a loud fit of angry arguing, each trying to speak over the other. They were interrupted by the sound of the door bursting open.

In the doorway stood a flustered woman in green robes. She was sweating excessively and red-faced, one hand clutching her heart and one hand tightly grasping the frame of the door for support as she wheezed.

"Gaia!" the council shouted in unison.

"The witch...sector three...," Councillor Gaia wheezed, too exhausted to get her words out properly.

She'd clearly been running for quite a while. She needed

a minute.

"What's the matter with sector three?" Zephyr asked, rising from his seat.

"Are the Terras in danger? We must send in troops immediately," Vulcan said.

"Right. I suppose we finally agree on something. Get the general in here," Marina said.

Gaia looked up, her eyes weary. "I'm afraid that won't be needed."

"Sorry?" Vulcan questioned.

"I thought you said sector three was in danger," Marina said, clearly annoyed. No one had time for this.

"That isn't the problem," Gaia said quietly, staring at her sodden boots.

"Then what is?!" Vulcan cried.

Gaia crossed her arms over her stomach and looked up at her fellow council members.

"Sector three is gone. The witch wiped it off the map."

Chapter 1
I Bid Farewell to a Bunch of Buildings

My heart felt like lead as I walked down a path that I have taken hundreds of times. My knees threatened to collapse from under me, but I urged myself to keep walking. I continued down the paved pathway and lifted my head upwards.

I continued walking down the paved pathway until I was standing a few meters from the Scribe Tower. The Scribe Tower was made from stone blocks and loomed hundreds of stories tall. In less than twenty-four hours, I would go inside the Scribe Tower where a Scribe would decide my fate. Standing in front of such a daunting building caused my vision to blur slightly and my head became foggy with a mixture of emotions and thoughts.

I knew I should feel excited. That's what everyone else felt the day before their induction. But in my disarray, one emotion is like a flashing light in my head. Fear. I realized that I had a tingle of fear of the unknown. In less than twenty four hours, I would go inside the Scribe Tower and figure out what power I have.

Embers control fire, Aquas control water, Auras control air, and Terras control Earth. Ever since I have known the concept of powers I have dreamed of being an Ember like my parents. The ability to control fire fascinated me far more than most people realize.

I turn around and walk towards the Ember School. The Ember School is the place I would train at if I became an Ember. I've always wanted to go into the Ember School, but rules are rules and the rules say only Embers are allowed inside. I have not visited the other sectors in years, so I haven't seen the other schools in a while.

Yawning, I turned to head home, saying goodbye to a few more familiar faces and buildings along the way. When I got home, I slipped off my shoes and climbed into my bed. I stared blankly at the ceiling for a few hours, letting my thoughts overwhelm me. Slowly, I closed my eyes and drifted off to sleep.

※※※

The next day I jolted awake from another nightmare. With sweat drenching my body through my shirt, I groggily wiped my eyes with the back of my hand. Light seeped through the small window from the corner of my room. I glanced towards the clock in the far corner of my bedroom. I'm forced to wipe my eyes once again to see the small hands.

11:00 am. Late. I quickly threw on a pair of red pants

and an orange shirt. The traditional Ember colors. Still slipping into my orange shoes, I burst out the door. I launched into a sprint hoping that the induction hadn't started yet. As I ran, buildings and trees blurred past me and my dirty blonde hair streamed behind me. Breathing heavily, I came to a stop outside of the Scribe Tower's looming doors. With one final deep breath, I opened the stone doors and walked inside.

chapter 2
I Get My Powers, Sort Of

I heard a faint mumble coming from the initiation room. Then silence. "Robyn, descendant of two Embers, please step forward." The voice seemed impatient.

My parents were both Embers, so I already knew that I should be one. But apparently I needed a scribe to confirm that, so there I was. I already lived in the Ember village, so with luck, I wouldn't have to move anywhere new. Well, I guess I wasn't one hundred percent sure that I would become a true Ember but I was still pretty sure, kind of, so that's good enough.

A guard was positioned on either side of the door holding a pole looking thing. They each had a vacant expression on their face, just looking straight forward, not blinking at all. I wondered if they were fake. I stood in front of one of them staring at them. Not blinking.

"Robyn please do not have a staring contest with the guards." Scribe Fallon sighed, never thinking she would ever have to say that. "We have things to do and very little time to do them."

"Yes, Scribe Fallon. Sorry, Scribe Fallon." I looked away from the guard and at Scribe Fallon.

I couldn't help myself from looking around the room. It was gorgeous. It was a huge room which was a bit odd because there was very little decoration in most of it. There was a grand fireplace with some flowers in vases and aroma diffusers on top. The walls were covered in see-through colored scarves. There were no windows so the only light came from the fireplace and the very few candles were placed on the floor in some parts of the room. In front of the fireplace was a rug (far enough back that it wouldn't catch on fire). The rug was extremely detailed with many different designs.

On the rug were two stools. One more grand than the other. That must be the scribe's stool. In Between the two stools was a small table. It was circular and made from the same frosted glass that was in the door. On it was a stone mortar and pestle, and a few vials of mysterious liquids. There was a spot on the wall with no scarf. It was a two by two box engraved into the wall. In each box was one of the four types of magic symbols. A flame for the Embers, a water droplet for the Aquas, A tree for the Terras and a cloud for the Auros.

"Hello? Robyn?" Scribe Fallon asked me.

"Huh, sorry I guess I zoned out," I replied, a little embarrassed.

"As I said Robyn, we have things to do and very little time to do them."

"Yep, sorry Scribe Fallon."

She led me to the two stools near the fireplace. "Sit!" she commanded.

Just like I had guessed, she sat on the grand stool. One of the motionless guards marched over to Scribe Fallon and whispered in her ear. "Oh yes I see... yes tell Serona her Initiation will have to be a bit later because someone-" Scribe Fallon looked directly at me "-isn't focusing."

"I know, I know I get off track easily but I'm sorry."

"It's alright but we really must be getting a move on with this."

The guard went back towards the door but instead of taking his usual place beside it, he opened the door and stood out there for about ten seconds before coming back and becoming motionless once again. He was most likely talking to "Serona" about the news. I didn't even know who that was, but whatever. As the Scribe said, we had things to do and obviously very little time to do them.

"Hands," Scribe Fallon ordered.

My hands were outstretched, hovering just above the small circular table. Scribe Fallon grabbed them very gently with her two hands and looked directly into my eyes. I tried to look away but something was compelling me to keep staring. Scribe Fallon broke eye contact and released my hands.

"So what am I? Are we done? Can I go now?" I wanted to be done with this.

"In a relationship the only way to trust is to not ask too many questions. Just trust that I will tell you anything you need to know. And no, we are not done yet," Scribe

Fallon's words were powerful.

She pulled the mortar and pestle closer to her and started adding some ingredients from the vials. To my surprise some of them were not liquids. Some were more of a powder. After adding about seven ingredients, Scribe Fallon looked up and said, "Now."

One of the guards had snuck up behind me and pulled out a hair from my head. He also handed me an empty vial and said, "Spit".

I have never heard his voice before. It was raspy, yet soothing and harsh, yet calm.

I did just as he said. The guard handed the vial and my hair to the scribe and went back beside the door. Scribe Fallon added my spit and hair to the concoction and started mixing with the pestle. It turned into some sort of thick liquid. She scooped it up with her hands and closed her eyes.

Suddenly Scribe Fallon opened her eyes very wide. She looked worried and almost even scared. The liquid disappeared in her hands. "Robyn you are... you have... you can..."

The Scribe could not finish her sentence. Abruptly, Scribe Fallon got up and hurried towards the guards. I couldn't quite hear what she was saying but the guards replied with a "Yes Scribe Fallon." Then they left and the Scribe stared at me.

I got up to ask what was going on but she pushed the air with her hands which sent me flying back to my seat. I tried again but she pushed me away again. Scribe Fallon seemed like she wanted to be separated from me. *Hurry up guards,* I heard a voice saying. It sounded like the Scribe's voice, but her mouth wasn't moving.

"Why do you need the guards?" I questioned.

"What how did... I didn't... What?" She was extremely confused, for she had said nothing.

I heard four sets of footsteps marching down the hall towards this room. Just like I thought, four guards had entered the room and were coming towards me. Two of them grabbed my arms while another stood behind me and the final guard who had told me to spit into the vial stood in front of me leading the way.

"STOP! Where are you taking me?" I tried to wiggle free but their grasps were too hard to break.

"DON'T RESIST," Scribe Fallon yelled.

I didn't listen. I kept trying to break free. Normally not obeying a scribe would get you severely punished but right now, I didn't care. I was trying extremely hard to break free until I did. I ran. Ran as fast as I could, but it wasn't enough. The guards caught up with me and this time they all were holding on to me. I gave up. There was no way I could escape this.

"What is happening?!" I screamed. A single teardrop fell down my cheek. My eyes were now clouded with tears. They loosened their grip just a little and brought me back to the room, closing the door behind me.

"I'm afraid we cannot say anything. The less you know the better," Scribe Fallon started. "Remember when I said to just trust me? And that I would tell you anything you need to know?"

"Yes," I calmed down a little. No more tears and screaming.

No more guards grabbing me and not letting go.

"You two can go now," the Scribe pointed at the two extra guards. "We shouldn't need you anymore."

"Thank you," I was forcing that out of my mouth. I wasn't in the mood for talking and felt like sitting alone, staring at the beautifully covered wall. Scribe Fallon seemed to understand that. She ushered the two guards away and followed them.

After a few minutes, they came back. I was fully calmed down by then. The guards went back to their post beside the door and Scribe Fallon led me to the door.

"Wait just a moment," the Scribe said, then hurried back towards the fireplace.

Scribe Fallon had reached into the fire. Normally she would probably get badly burned but when she took her arm out not only was it unscathed, but was also holding a very small wooden box. The wood should've burned. She should've burned. The only people that could reach into fire and come out unharmed, were the Embers, but Scribe Fallon wasn't an Ember, she was... a... a... well she was a Scribe. They weren't considered Embers, Aquas, Terras, or Auras. They could just feel what other peoples powers were and obviously had some basic powers, nothing too special.

That made me think. Everything must be under control. I bet what was happening is that I didn't get Fire powers. Both my parents were Embers, so maybe she also thought I would become one too, but maybe I didn't. If this was true, I really hoped I wouldn't become an Aqua because that would be like betraying my family. Embers and Aquas were natural enemies.

Wait no that's crazy, I thought. *This stuff happens sometimes and the Scribes don't freak out over that at all. This must be something worse. Much much worse.*

Scribes were trained to go through and deal with anything that might happen or go wrong. They were trained to act calm, so then why was Scribe Fallon going crazy?

"Come sit, Robyn," Scribe Fallon said. "Do you know what this is?" She held out the box. I saw her arm. It was not unscathed at all. In fact it looked bright red with a few minor scratches.

"Um no, but are you okay? Your arm, it's…"

"Yes I am fine. As a Scribe I am trained to withstand any and all harsh conditions."

"I understand, but you literally reached your hand into fire."

"I know, I know, but I'm fine."

Scribe Fallon mixed together two vials into a paste and spread it across her arm. The redness and scratches disappeared within seconds.

"In this box are tests. I will need you to complete them."

I was worried. What if the tests were hard and painful? The Scribe turned towards the guards. "Cancel all my appointments for today." Then, she whispered. "This might take a while."

The box contained eight things. A candle, a lighter, a cup, a bottle of water, a pedestal, a vase, a pot with soil, and finally a pack of seeds. First she put the pot with soil and the pack of seeds on the table.

"You will put a seed in the pot and try to grow it into a fully grown flower."

I placed one seed and covered it with soil. I tried everything

I could think of to try and grow the flower. Nothing happened.

"I see, now pour water from this bottle into this cup and try to control it." Scribe Fallon removed the pot and seeds off the table and replaced it with the bottle of water and cup.

I poured the water and again, tried everything I could to move the water. Nothing happened.

"Interesting. Now place this vase on top of this pedestal and try to push it off without touching it. For the third time I tried everything I could to try and make the vase move. Nothing happened.

"Okay now light this candle with this lighter and try to make the fire grow with your hands." The scribe replaced the pedestal and vase with a candle and lighter.

I was sure I could do this one because I was a descendant of Embers. I lit the candle and tried to make the fire grow. Nothing again.

Scribe Fallon opened her eyes so wide, I was sure they were stuck.

No no this can't be happening. I don't understand. I heard Scribe Fallon's voice but her mouth wasn't moving again, "What don't you understand?"

"What the?!?!"

"Just calm down." As soon as I said that, she had in fact calmed down.

"What are you doing to me?" she yelled.

"Nothing. I'm not doing anything to you." Just then

I realized that there was something strange going on. Something neither I nor the scribe could understand.

"We need to go. NOW!"

She led me towards the doors. Luckily, this time the guards stayed put. No one grabbed me, she just led me out. It was nice. I finally felt in control. Well not *in control* but I felt like I had control over myself somewhat.

The doors slammed behind us which startled me very much. The guards had come out, but not to grab me but to stand guard outside of the doors. I got nervous for a second but since they were not following us, I felt much better.

Chapter 3
I Get Taken to Prison

I followed Scribe Fallon through town, still trying to comprehend what had just happened. The Scribe said she needed to "Escort me somewhere," but I wasn't told anything else. Where was I being taken? I hadn't even been told what my elemental power was! Scribe Fallon was just about to tell me when I noticed the concerned look on her face. The next thing I knew, I was being taken somewhere. I didn't even bother asking where we were going… because I'd already asked her repeatedly and I got no answer.

As we were walking through the streets, I noticed that we were heading towards the quiet part of town. She led me through an area that was notably less wealthy, with derelict buildings and homeless people huddled around an oil drum fire. I recognized this area as it was home to the town's prison. This wasn't just a regular prison, this was The Maximum Security Prison in Sector 3, where only the most dangerous criminals were held.

It was a large grey stone building. I heard that nothing in the building was made of wood, in case the prisoners tried to burn things down. The structure was old, but it was definitely strong. Not even the green vines that ran down the sides of the building got damaged in storms. On the outside, the prison was heavily guarded. There were armed guards surrounding the whole building, and there was an electric fence around the outside. Despite having an electric fence, there was no prison yard. Not a lot of information about this prison was shared with the public, but I was pretty sure that they had an indoor gym somewhere in there so that the prisoners could stay fit and healthy. As notable as the reputation of its inmates, no one had ever been able to escape.

I thought we were heading in the direction of the prison, but then the Scribe turned down a dimly lit, uninviting alleyway. Why on earth would we need to be here? The alley smelled awful, and besides us, there was no one or nothing in it but a couple of trash cans. I couldn't understand why I was being led through here, but Scribes were sagacious and I had to respect them. So I did my best to trust her, as I followed her through the alley.

We walked down the alleyway until we reached a dead end. Great. We'd walked all this way for nothing.

I stood there while the Scribe searched her pocket for something. She pulled out an odd-looking stone that had a strange symbol engraved into it. I watched in curiosity while the Scribe took the stone, and pressed it against the wall of the alley. I was quite confused, but before I could think about what was going to happen, something incredible occurred. The stone wall lit up and started to break into little pieces of rock. The stone wall crumbled to the ground, revealing something mysterious.

A staircase.

A cobblestone staircase that led underground.

This journey that the Scribe was taking me on was finally becoming interesting.

She gestured for me to walk down the staircase, so I took one step inside and waited for her to come with me. I watched as the Scribe pressed her stone against one of the pieces of what was left of the stone wall. She stood next to me and watched the entrance. Seconds later, the wall started to repair itself, until it looked like it had never been broken; leaving me and the Scribe standing in a pitch-black stairwell.

"Watch your step" mumbled the Scribe as she began to walk down the stairs.

Watch my step? I couldn't walk down a staircase in this light! I was about to argue about it with her but then realized that she was already halfway down the stairs. I carefully began to walk down, making sure not to slip, or bump into the Scribe.

When we reached the end of the staircase, we found ourselves in a small room. It was still dark, but I was just able to make out the Scribe's face. I saw her reach for something that was mounted against the wall. She took the stone back out of her pocket and held it near the object she'd just grabbed. The stone glowed red, and then suddenly set on fire. She used the stone to light a torch, which was apparently the object she'd found.

Now that I could finally see, I looked around the room we were in. The walls and floors were stone, and there were a few torches mounted on the wall. I turned to my left to notice a long, narrow hallway, so long that I couldn't see what was at the end.

The Scribe lit a second torch and handed it to me. I pointed it at the hallway entrance, but I still couldn't see what was at the end. She put her stone back into her pocket and gestured for me to follow her. She began to lead me down the hallway. I thought about the stone she had, I wondered what else it could do.

"Where'd you get the stone from?" I asked, even though I didn't expect an answer.

"It's a stone given to all Scribes so they can access special places," the Scribe replied.

"Special places like what?" I inquired. She didn't reply. We continued to walk down the hallway. The only smell was the damp walls that surrounded us. The only sounds were the echoes of our footsteps tapping against the stone floor.

Finally, I could see the end of the hallway. There was a big door to the right and a stairwell to the left. I looked up the staircase, wondering what it led to.

"We're here," the Scribe proclaimed. She drew my attention to the large iron door. She then used her stone to unlock it, (apparently, this stone could do everything). She led me inside the room and I held up my torch so I could get a better look at my surroundings. The room slightly resembled a cave, as the walls and floor were made of unevenly placed stones.

On the Other Side

I walked further into the room and noticed there were several more torches on the wall, I used mine to light them all. Now that the room was fully lit, I was able to see everything around me. Before I took a proper look around, I remembered that the Scribe was still here with me. I turned around to see that she was about to exit the room. She gave me a nod and then left.

"So I guess I'm on my own now..."

I continued to walk around the room, wondering why the Scribe brought me here. The room had a damp and musty odor, but other than that, nothing here really stood out to me. I kept walking further into the room, there were no torches to light anymore, so I could only use the one I was holding.

Then I saw something strange. It looked like a prison cell. Thick iron bars stretched from one side of the room to the other. I held my torch closer, wondering if anyone was kept here in the cell.

"Hello?" I called.

"I've been waiting for you, Robyn," a voice replied.

The voice was gravelly, and rather unsettling if I was being honest.

"How do you know my name?" I asked.

I waited for a reply, but instead, I heard footsteps coming toward me. I held up my torch and noticed a rather old man walking in my direction.

"I've been waiting for your arrival for quite some time now," he said.

"That wasn't really the answer to my question," I mumbled.

The man came closer to the bars of his cell. He was tall and thin and had grey hair and blue-grey eyes. His skin was wrinkly and pale, and he wore tattered clothing. There was a smile on his face, yet he still seemed very lugubrious.

"You're a very special child Robyn."

A special child? Me?

"I'm actually not sure what I'm doing here. I don't even know where I am! I was supposed to find out what my elemental power was, and then I was taken here." I told him.

"Well first off," the man explained, "you are currently underneath the Maximum Security Prison.."

"Really?" I exclaimed.

"Yes, my cell is in the basement, a gloomy and rather depressing place to be honest," he said. "They kept me down here because they say that I'm too dangerous to be kept around other inmates."

"Why are you *too dangerous*?" I asked. The man chuckled but didn't say anything. "Who are you anyway?" I inquired.

"I'm a very powerful person," he proclaimed.

If he was so powerful, then why was he in prison? He was clearly being held here in this prison cell and- "Oh my gosh this is a prison cell. Am I talking to a criminal?!" I exclaimed.

How could I have forgotten that since this was a prison cell, then obviously the person being held here was bad?

"Criminal or not my dear, you still need me," the man grinned.

I crossed my arms. "Why would I need you? How can

I even trust you? You're a criminal, you may *say* that you're powerful, but how can I believe that?"

"Aren't you wondering why you've been brought here?" he chortled. "The only reason you're here is so you can talk to me!" Even though what the man was saying seemed to make sense, I was still confused.

"Why would I need to talk to you?" I queried.

"Well just like I said before, you're special." The prisoner sat down on the stone floor and gestured for me to do the same. I held the torch closer to the iron bars, so we were able to see each other. The prisoner cleared his throat. "Alright Robyn, let me tell you what's going on.

"See, you've heard of the four elemental powers, Fire, Air, Earth, and Water, but there is a fifth power that people rarely talk about, as it's quite uncommon for people to obtain."

"What's the fifth power?" I asked.

"I'm getting to that, don't be so impatient," the prisoner snapped. "Once, a young boy discovered that he had a power no one else had gotten before. Mind control. As well as emotion control. It took him a while to learn about his powers, as he had to figure everything out on his own. But eventually, the young boy became an expert at mind and emotion control."

I looked at his sunken eyes, "It's you isn't it?" I asserted. "The boy who had the powers."

He nodded slowly and grasped the cold prison bars with his hands. "This is a power to be taken seriously, Robyn. Being able to control people's emotions, and actually being able to control people, is a very powerful thing that must be used wisely.

"It's dangerous to have so much power, so dangerous that you could possibly end up like me," he admitted.

"What do you mean, *I* could end up like you?" I hesitated.

"Don't you see? Don't you now understand why you weren't told your power at the Ceremony? Don't you know why you are here talking to *me*?" the prisoner implied.

I thought about it for a minute. What he was saying couldn't be true. Both my parents were Embers, so I was sure that I must be as well. "Do I have mind control powers?"

"Now you get it!" exclaimed the man.

I stared at him blankly. I didn't understand how this could be. Anyone could have gotten these powers, but it just so happened to be me? Me? Of all people.

Wow. I imagined all of the things I could do with this. I could change people's opinions about me! I could make people do whatever I wanted them to!

"How do I use these powers?" I asked, excitedly.

"It's not that easy, you know," the prisoner informed me. "It takes a lot of practice and strength to get good at mind control."

"I'll do whatever it takes," I boasted.

"Then take this," the prisoner handed me a stone. Though not just any stone, the same one as the Scribe that took me here had. "Come here every day at the same time as you did today. I'll teach you everything you need to know about mind and emotion control."

I nodded and stood up. I thanked the man for everything and promised to return tomorrow.

I began to walk out of the room, extinguishing the torches as I went. I used the stone to lock the iron door, and I walked down the long hallway, and back up the staircase. I used the stone once more, to open and then close the exit. I stepped back into the dingy alleyway and began to walk back home.

❊❊❊

The next day, I went back to see the Prisoner again. On my way there, I thought about everything that had happened yesterday. I couldn't wrap my head around the fact that I had mind and emotion control. I could do so many things with these powers. Clearly, I was very excited to learn how to use my powers.

When I arrived at the prison, we wasted no time. The Prisoner immediately began to teach me about my powers.

"Little is known about our gift," the Prisoner mentioned. "But I've spent my whole life figuring out as much as I can about it." The Prisoner began to tell me all about how to work my powers. He said that I would have to concentrate really hard on what I wanted someone to do or feel. If I could stay focused, and concentrate as much as I could, then it should work.

The Prisoner and I mostly talked about how I could use my powers before I was allowed to practice. "Ok, now try and make me happy," he instructed. I focused hard on what I needed to do, yet unfortunately it was unsuccessful.

For the whole week, I came to see the prisoner, and everyday I practiced my powers.

One day, after many attempts, I made the prisoner lift his right arm!

"Very well done," he'd said. "Keep practicing!"

And so I did.

chapter 4
A Lady Says A Lot of Words

That day I decided I would go and practice on my own. Just to make sure all this training was actually doing something. I should probably check in with my master, but I figured I wouldn't miss much if I did it early enough.

I woke up that morning and got dressed as usual. Blue jeans, a black t-shirt, and a flannel sweater in case it got chilly - no longer in Ember colors.

I looked at myself in the mirror. My shoulder-length hair, and olive skin. My face was more feminine, more structured, with full lips, but my body was long and lean.

It was cold. As soon as I stepped out my door I was hit by the morning mist of mid-March.

Man, it's brisk out here, I thought to myself.

I took the button-up sweater from around my waist and wrapped it around me. I looked around. I could sense the muddled emotions of the people around me. Stumbling groggily down the street at this early hour, hot coffee in hand. Walking to wherever they needed to be.

I grabbed a tuque from inside. As I walked I passed piles of slush, slowly melting as the sun continued to creep upwards, illuminating the gray sky. Although it happened every morning, I still loved how the sun broke through the clouds, and shone like light from heaven through the barren branches.

I realized people were staring. I was stared at regularly, just because I was who I was. Though this was more or less because I had stopped to close my eyes and look at the sun, the warm rays on my face. I could have stopped anywhere, so I stopped right in the middle of the sidewalk. I guessed that may have looked weird.

I smiled and waved at the gawking strangers, just to show them that I didn't care what they thought of me. Well, I did, but they didn't have to know that. Even though they didn't know me personally. Despite how confidential my powers were supposed to be, word must have seeped out. People knew about a non-binary teen with non-elemental magical powers. Sure *some* people were accepting, and I valued those *some*.

Yet still, it was only some. No matter how much time might have passed, equality didn't seem to fit in. Like me.

I continued to walk to the park. Several benches were placed around a dry central fountain. I sat alone. A few people were there. Old and young. It wasn't super popular, but I liked it. I chose to come *here* because this place was safe ground. People from every tribe, Aquas, Terras, Auras, and Embers could come here and enjoy a lovely afternoon. They couldn't outlaw hostile language but it was sort of a given.

This was a place where no matter your magical background, you could come here and drink some tea, and not be bothered.

But I wanted to bother these people.

I looked around the mossy cobblestone landing, threaded with small, leafless oak trees, and began to choose my target.

I ate my bagel while going over the steps in my head. *1. Search the emotions. 2. Find a place of vulnerability. 3. Think about what you want them to do. 4. Persuade them to do so.* It was more complex than that, but if you really boiled it down, that was the gist.

I picked someone in the distance, oh no, wait... Yep, that was a statue. Okay, maybe a living being?

A little girl. She might work.

I listened to her emotions. I felt happy, as I watched the little girl try and tell the fountain to "spill". Which I guessed meant she wanted the water to run, or she wanted the fountain to tell her its secrets.

I didn't know, but her father thought it was hilarious. He was sitting on the bench with, what seemed to be his son, slapping his knee and saying to his daughter: "It's too cold right now, honey."

I smiled. I missed that.

I chose the action I wanted her to do. I really, really tried to persuade her to start tapping her right foot. Perhaps in thought about what she could do to make the fountain *spill*. But she just... didn't.

I tried and tried, changed out the actions, and even

tried different people.

At some point, when no one would respond, I may have just yelled aloud, "Raise your left hand, old lady!"

At that point, the old lady sitting on a seat near mine, still didn't. Was she another statue? She didn't even flinch. She just sighed and stared wistfully at the fountain.

Wistfully.

I could use that. I latched on to her wistful feeling. Even though I didn't know why she felt wistful, wistfulness was easily converted into sadness. A sense of longing. See, when altering emotions you can't just go straight from happy to sad. Well, at least I couldn't. There had to be a transition, creating emotion.

I urged her gently to feel sad. I needed susceptibility.

I thought again, *Raise your left hand, C'mon just for fun.* And her left arm twitched. I continued persuading. *People might think it's weird, but you're like really old, so like, who cares.*

She had started to actually raise her hand before I said that last part. Maybe insulting people wasn't the best way to get people to do what you wanted them to. In that sense, it had worked for me before.

I tried again.

You miss somebody, I guessed.

The lady's eyes became glossy.

Did you love them? I didn't know much about love, but it seemed like the obvious follow-up.

I'm sure they loved you too. I had no idea if I was right or not. I could only sense emotions, not read minds and thoughts. Although, by the look in her eyes, I seemed to have hit a soft spot.

Raise your left hand, I thought again. *It might make you feel better.* Wow, convincing. But nonetheless, it worked.

The lady raised her left hand and smiled. She looked up to the sky and mouthed, *I miss you too.*

Wait? She thought I was the person she missed… speaking to her. I mean, she could believe whatever, but like, OK.

I felt elated. I had done it. Well, it was a start, but I still couldn't help but feel good.

It was fun, manipulating someone. Having them do exactly what you wanted them to do. This was all I had planned on doing today. My own expectations were met! Which now that I think about it, seemed very low.

BUCKET LIST

GET OLD LADY TO RAISE HER LEFT HAND

GET A LITTLE BOY TO SAY "HAPPY BIRTHDAY" TO HIS MOM.

Anyway, who was next?

I decided I would attempt a slightly harder target. A middle-aged man, from the water tribe, sitting and reading the newspaper. I figured this would be more challenging, because the more set in your ways you were, the harder it was to change.

Though I guessed if I was just asking him to scratch his temple, I doubted that that would be too difficult. I wasn't asking him to quit his job or believe in a different god. I just wanted him to scratch his temple.

His emotions weren't very vibrant, he seemed very focused on the issue he was reading. I thought about what

I wanted him to do.

Is your head itchy? What just brushed against your forehead? The cool breeze blew my dark blond hair over my face, breaking my focus. When I brushed it away the man had started to get up and leave.

Wait! I thought. *What is the title of the next article? Is it intriguing? Sit back down and read it before you go.*

He did indeed sit down. He looked at the paper, then his watch and grabbed a pen from his bag. He underlined something on the page, then got up and left. Stuffing the newspaper into his bag as he hurried off. I mean it had kinda worked…

I scanned the crowd. Nobody really evoked my attention this time. Not that it mattered, because a second later I keeled over and everything went black.

❉❉❉

I awoke in a room with four others. Though the room wasn't real. Black stone pillars lined a long hallway. The ceiling was raised about 40 feet in the air, coming to a peak at the top. The room was menacing in a way, but also beautiful. Everything seemed to be covered in a thick haze. My surroundings were still the same. I hadn't been transported anywhere. Through the transparency of the vision, I could still see the park when I really focused. It was kind of disorienting because I was lying on a bench so when I looked at the park my perspective changed. Everything was turned sideways.

Then I closed my eyes.

The room didn't go away, in fact, it became clearer. The others more present.

In the dim light, I couldn't make out their appearances all that well. The torches cast dark shadows across their faces and illuminated their hair. The firelight danced around us. They seemed just as confused as I was. Two girls, two boys, all about my age.

What had they been doing before this? I wondered.

I noticed that they were all looking at something. At the end of the hallway was an altar. A throne of that same dark rock atop a raised gold dais.

I realized where I was. I was in the Hall of Prophecies. Although it wasn't crumbling. It was in perfect condition. The thick dust that covered the floor was now gone. Not a spiderweb in sight. It was magical.

I had passed this place before but I was prohibited from going inside. This was where, in ancient times, the Prophet would give out quests to heroes, so that they could save the world from whatever danger they would come to face.

The Prophet was practically a god. They could predict the future through prophecies, they could see the past in perfect rendition, even if they weren't alive at the time. Our Prophet, Prophet Gizziah, was said to have lived for over a hundred years. She, like all ones before, was given the knowledge from all Prophets that came before her in a sacred ritual that was only known by a few of the eldest elementalists in each sector of the kingdom.

The Hall of Prophecies was the place where the Prophets of old issued prophecies and granted quests to the worthy.

"Alongside Air, water, earth, fire,
All whose presence's are indeed dire,
Is another whose gifts unknown,
The Ancient magic of mind control.

"Finally, a monster whose powers almighty,
Will soon divulge their plan for supremacy,
Band together for thou need fight,
So that the world shant plunge into eternal night."

I waited for her to continue. She did not.

Her aura vanished and she stood once again. She returned her hands to her chest and bowed her head. The torches faded back to normal and the smoke dissipated. The others and I exchanged nervous glances.

The Prophet spoke again.

"Younglings, alongside each other on this quest you shall form bonds unbreakable. So listen well. Ye need to meet again in the morning at this very place. For thou must commence your quest where it started.

"I may not be able to guide you along the way, for I must stay. But if I can say, look for the mountain that stands out of the way," she paused. "I must apologize for I cannot lead you further onward. Perhaps I have already said too much. The fate of the world rests on your success. I do not mean to pressure you, this quest leads you on your own journey, together. I hope you succeed, young ones. Ashen, Rune, Robyn, Nova, Valen, each of you will learn more about your gifts and the reason I chose you, but for now, I bid you farewell. Good luck."

On the Other Side

And then everything was gone.

❖❖❖

I opened my eyes to see the park where I was manipulating people just moments before. But it seemed different now. Or I felt different. Was this what it felt like to have a panic attack?

Those words just kept repeating in my head:

"Alongside air, water, earth, and fire,
All whose presences are indeed dire,
Is another whose gifts unknown,
The Ancient magic of mind control."

It wasn't a mistake, it couldn't be. I wished it was, but I couldn't *not* go to the Hall of Prophecies tomorrow. I couldn't ignore the words of this Prophet, *the* Prophet.

Tomorrow I would embark on a quest with Valen, Rune, Ashen, and Noah? No right *Nova.*

The rest of that day passed in a gloomy but frantic haze. I needed to come prepared the next day, but what did *prepared* entail? I bought a sword, a scabbard for my back, and some first aid stuff.

The sword was silver with a purple gri, gold accents and glass pommel (that nobbly thing at the end of the hilt I think). It looked wicked. That night I packed anything and everything that would fit into my backpack. Three changes of clothes, food, first aid, water, and anything else that would fit. I would wear my weapons on my person, you know, just in case.

I spent the next several hours lying awake in bed, The prophecy repeating over and over, watching the clock as it changed from 11:59 A.M to 12:00 A.M. In just 6 measly hours of sleep I would have to do what I dreaded, waking up. But on a very different morning.

It looked like I would miss training.

chapter 5
I Meet Fireboy and Watergirl

The Hall of Prophecies was in the center of all the sectors combined, equal distance for each one. I was far away.

Hooray! Running! I tied my shoelaces because I didn't want to trip and fall on my face. Trust me, it hurt, I knew from experience. And then, I started jogging.

Just kidding, after fifteen minutes, I was drenched in sweat and heavily breathing. So I sat down on the nearest bench and said to myself that when someone on a bicycle came by I would take it.

I was very pleased when one did. *OK, Robyn you got this.*

I walked into the middle of the sidewalk and stood there. As the little girl on her bike came closer, I tried to get inside her head and tell her to stop. But she kept going.

Did she not see me? Even without my powers, a normal person would stop. I kept trying to get her to stop. I blamed her helmet, it was probably the thing making getting in her head more difficult. Parents these days are so inconsiderate!

STOP!

And just as she was about to run into me, she didn't. She was there sitting on the purple non-moving bike.

Now get off.

I decided for her.

She got off the bike. "Thank you random little girl," and I pedaled off.

I heard her yell and start to cry. Sorry, but I was a tad more important at the moment.

I biked past houses, stores and many, many people. Who gave me looks. I didn't blame them. A sixteen-year-old riding a ten-year-old girl's bike would look pretty weird.

It took me a good half hour to get to the Hall of Prophecies because I was really bad at physical activity and I took a break in between to get a corndog (I was hungry and I passed a stand selling them on the way!) I ate it on the sidewalk with the bike I took beside me. Then I continued my journey across the city.

When I finally got there, I jumped off the bike and pushed it into the white brick wall. I walked up to the front doors of the building and tried opening them. But it wouldn't budge. I kept pulling at the door only to realize it said to push. I mentally slapped myself. *Great going, Robyn.*

I pushed the door open and entered the building. I realized that this was the first time I'd come here. I'd never had time to do this with my parents.

There were scrolls with prophecies of the past behind the glass, and pictures of the people that were on them. Someday that would be me.

Oh, and the others, of course. If they actually survived. By the stories behind some of these quests, things could get brutal. I searched the whole two-story building and couldn't find anyone. Then as I walked outside, about to give up, I heard voices:

"Nope, not happening!"

"Ugh why me?"

"Well, it's not my fault I got caught up in this. I didn't choose this."

Were some of the things I heard. I thought for a second. The prophecy said there would be four more people coming with me. So I followed the voices to the gardens behind the building. I passed a couple of statues of scribes and a fountain before I saw them.

There was a boy with blonde hair and red highlights, one with blonde hair, a girl with dark brown hair, and one with long black hair braided to her waist.

They seemed to be arguing. I was somewhat hidden behind some bushes filled with white flowers. I kept listening to them argue but a bee flew into my face. I tried shooing it away quietly but failed miserably. The boy with blonde hair and red highlights pointed me out.

"Who are you and what are you doing here?" he asked as a bit of fire appeared in his palms and the other kids turned to look at me.

"Well, you see.."

"Get to it already" the girl with black hair said, crossing

her arms into her chest.

"OK. My name is Robyn, and I was told to come here by some illusion prophet lady." I quickly explained. They looked at each other. I slowly walked up to them. The red-haired boy still had fire in his palms. I rolled my eyes.

Put the fire out. And sit down.

I took control and he did as he was told. The others looked at me as if I were an alien.

Not surprising.

"So you're the girl that has different powers than everyone else " the black-haired girl sneered.

And I looked at her.

"You got a problem with that?" I looked her up and down. She was wearing a navy blue top and white jean shorts. "Watergirl, I imagine."

She nodded her head.

"Fireboy," I asked the one with blonde hair highlighted red. He also nodded.

Fireboy and Watergirl, I used to play that game. It was fun. Naturally, I was Fireboy because I was raised by people who could control fire. But that was beside the point.

I looked at the other two, raising an eyebrow. The dark-skinned brunette opened up her palm and started making some dirt move in it. And the other blonde boy started waving his hand. A small gust of wind went in my face. *Okay, thanks for that.*

"So," the brunette started. "I guess we will be going on a quest together." Mostly everyone rolled their eyes.

Hey, I'm the freak here! I'm the only one with super rare powers to control the mind and emotions of other people!

They kept looking at each other angrily, so I did the best I could and I tried to calm them down.

CALM DOWN AND SIT!

Their faces soon relaxed and they sat down on the ground. *Thank you, powers.* I followed and sat between watergirl and fireboy.

"Where were you when you got the prophecy?" I asked them.

Fireboy started, "Well, I was having lunch at the steak house with my family when I got it. I was just eating my steak with barbeque sauce and fries and nodding my head, pretending to care about what everyone else was talking about and -*BAM!*- illusion lady appeared, and scared me half to death too. I choked on a fry. And after they were done talking I rushed out of the restaurant and left my steak there. Oh, my parents also!"

He had been waving his hands as he explained and as a consequence of sitting beside him, I got slapped in the face.

"Hey, watch where you wave those things!" I yelled at him. He looked at me and rolled his eyes.

"Who's next?" I looked around the circle.

Blondie decided to speak up. "I was hanging out with a couple friends in the park. They were skateboarding and I was filming them doing all their tricks, because they asked me to and I didn't mind not skating, and well halfway through I got the prophecy. I dropped their camera and ran here after." He said, "And now I owe them a camera, it probably broke. Gosh, those things are really expensive!" he sighed in disappointment.

Next, the dark-skinned brunette: "I was in the park reading a book about earth substances and then as you two said, I saw this illusion of the prophet. They told me the prophecy and that I was to come here, where I would meet you guys and start the quest. I made my way over as quickly as I could and heard the boys talking." She sighed.

I turned to the black-haired girl. "Your turn," I declared.

"Well, I was out getting ice cream with my best friend."

"Ice cream!" Fireboy laughed. Watergirl looked at him with confusion.

"Why is that funny?" she asked him.

"You know you control water, there is ice in ice cream. Ice is water," he said.

"There is absolutely nothing funny about that," she responded, annoyed. "But anyway, I was eating ice cream at this little cafe with my friend. I went to the bathroom and as I was, you know, going to the bathroom, and it just appeared out of nowhere telling me everything it told you guys. So here I am."

Now everyone was looking at me. It was my turn to tell them my story, and I did. It was then that I realized that I didn't even know whose name was whose. I quickly asked. And I got this:

Fireboy was named Ashen.

Watergirl was Nova.

Miss I read books about my Powers, Rune.

And blondie was Valen.

Ashen was fire, Nova was water, Rune was earth and Valen was air.

The fact that we all had different powers wasn't really

great. Sure there wasn't war between the different powers but there had been a lot of violent encounters recently.

I sighed. It was worse that I had the powers I had because only one other person had ever had them, and they were locked in a high-security cell.

I didn't want that to be me. I would avoid that at all costs. So if I had to go on a quest with a bunch of prissies, so be it.

All I knew was that this was going to be a very long quest.

chapter 6
Maybe This Quest is A Bad Idea

"**Maybe this quest is a bad idea,**" Nova said. "Lots of dangerous things can happen, haven't you heard other stories about what happens to other groups when they go on a quest?"

"No," I responded, paying half the attention that I should have been.

"There was this one group, around the same age as us who had the same prophecy. When they headed out, each of the 5 of them headed in different directions and they didn't stick together. They always fought and never agreed on anything. Each one of them did their own thing so eventually they all got separated from each other and got lost and no one knows what happened to them."

The prophecy brought us here, why would it tell us we need to do this if we don't need to? And besides, we'll stick together then," I responded, quite annoyed at Nova for bringing this up.

"Yeah I mean, we have to do it because it must be for an important reason, but it can be very dangerous if we aren't careful," Rune said.

Ashen was awfully quiet. He seemed uncomfortable in the situation and looked like he wanted to say something but didn't at the same time.

"Ashen, are you okay? You're really quiet," I asked.

"No, I'm not okay." Ashen rose from where he was sitting and raised his voice louder than needed. "You don't even belong in the four power groups, I have fire, Nova has water, Rune earth, and Valen air. You have some weird controlling powers that are really dangerous. You shouldn't be here and you are not going to come along with us on this quest."

I was in complete shock. "You don't get to decide if I am coming on this quest, the prophecy brought us here, it brought all of us here, you don't get to decide."

"Then the prophecy sure made a mistake," Ashen said.

I lost it. Without thinking, I went after him. I wanted to beat him into the ground. What gave him the right to talk about my powers? He didn't have them, he didn't understand them.

Nova and Valen broke us up. I was filled up with anger. I didn't know why, but it made me so mad. I wasn't one to get mad over silly things. Ashen just really pushed my bubble.

After a whole twenty minutes of silence, Nova spoke up.

"You guys, we have to work together. We were brought together for a reason, not to fight. The prophecy wanted us to do something together, it needs us five to figure something out. I'm not completely sure what, but without us working together we won't be able to solve the mystery,"

"Now how about you both apologize and we get on preparing for the quest?"

"We still need to train our powers and get all our necessities in check," I spoke up even though I really didn't want to. "I'm sorry Ashen."

"I'm sorry too, I didn't mean it so harshly, it was just on my mind. And I agree with Nova. We were brought together for a reason so we have to work together."

The discussion was over.

❊❊❊

We started training our powers for the big quest. There was no question we would need to use them. Ashen practiced his fire powers by lighting a candle and making a fire using his mind. Nova practiced her water powers by making water show in a water bottle and also by growing water plants. Rune practiced her power by controlling plants, rocks and dirt. Valen then trained his air powers by aeroportating which was teleporting using the wind.

Then it was finally my turn. I focused really hard on Valen. I wanted to control his emotions and thoughts and I knew that the only way of doing so was if I concentrated as the Prisoner had taught me.

Everyone was silent, they knew how much concentration this power required. I focused hard, harder than I had done in the past two weeks.

I focused on making Valen mad, I wanted to make sure that what I was doing really worked.

If I tried to make him happy, I wouldn't know if I made him happy or if he was just happy before, after all Valen is very positive and never really gets mad at anyone.

I concentrated on making him mad at Ashen. Even though he had apologized, I still had this anger that needed to come out at him.

I was, for the first time, successful on the first try. I guess I had been really mad at Ashen. Valen walked over to Ashen and gave him a really hard punch in the stomach. I didn't know I had made him that mad.

"Oh my... What in the world, Robyn?" Nova asked, jumping in shock.

"It worked! It worked!" I chanted, filled with so much excitement.

"What the hell?" Ashen said, raging.

"Sorry Ashen, I'm so sorry," I said, still happy on the inside.

"Okay, now we keep practicing so that we are confident when we need to really use them," Rune suggested, trying to change the subject.

So we did, we practiced our powers all evening, taking no breaks. When sundown came, we got everything ready and went to bed.

Tomorrow the journey would really begin and we had no idea what was about to happen.

chapter 7
Open Sesame

Two Days Later

I rubbed the sleep out of my eyes as I slowly woke up in a sleeping bag on the ground. Stupid prophecy. So vague and confusing.

I didn't even know what the point of this was. I looked around at my sleeping "teammates" (ha) as I thought about the prophecy again.

We had to head north and supposedly find this special tower with some ancient magician guide? I thought it was called the Tower of Secrets. *Wow, such an original name!* I just loved the creativity.

I sat up and checked my watch. The time was 6:11 AM.

We were supposed to leave at sunrise, which was in about half an hour. Stupid specifics in stupid prophecies making me wake up. Ugh.

I decided to try and persuade Ashen to wake up because I was bored. I concentrated and reached out and thought into his brain: *WAKE UP!*

He literally jumped out of his sleeping bag and smacked his head on the side of the tent, cursing.

I smirked and he gave me a death glare after determining what had happened. He was so alert after my "wake up" that he looked like a fire alarm went off in his ear.

He looked around rapidly at our sleeping teammates and checked his watch and folded his sleeping bag and sipped some water, all the while glaring at me. I was nearly on the verge of laughing.

I decided to let the others stay sleeping a little longer. Ashen went out to go running to let out some of his energy. I chuckled as he took off like an Olympic sprinter towards the border mountains.

We were on the edge of the main kingdom, and we were about to cross the border. The Tower was about two miles and a half past the border mountains. We would have to make it past the mountains and travel to the Tower to start our quest.

This quest was so confusing. We had barely started and most of the prophecy didn't make sense. We were supposed to go to this Tower of Secrets and get guidance from this ancient dude. Then we had a traitor in our group or something.

The rest of the group started to wake up, interrupting my thoughts.

Nova walked up to me, blinked groggily and wrinkled her nose at me. "Ew, take a shower sometime. You need to do something about your wardrobe."

I glared at her as she opened her bag and grabbed her things.

Dang, she was so annoying! She was so rude and stuck-up. She had such a big head just because she figured out the first line of the prophecy. The water tribe had legends about an ancient magician who lived in the tower north.

She thought she was *so* superior and was just so cocky about everything. She was also so impulsive and barely thought about anything before leaping into battle like a maniac. She was too sarcastic as well. We could barely talk without her injecting some kind of sarcasm into every other sentence.

We fought some monsters on our way out of the border and took them out pretty easily. The only good thing was that the monsters were now keeping their distance.

I woke everyone up (nicely) and a few minutes later, we were ready. Everyone got their things and I folded up the tent and stuffed it in my bag. Ashen sprinted back to us, looking a bit less awake, but he looked like he could still run a while without breaking a sweat.

Valen and Rune looked at me questioningly. I shook my head with a smile. I led the way to our next stop, a small secret pass through the border mountains. We left the actual border of the kingdom a mile or two back, but the border mountains were as far as anyone had ever gone.

Yippee! We'd be the first people to die past the border mountains.

We reached the first mountain a little bit after 8 AM. I quickly decided that this wasn't the mountain we were looking for. It was too normal. The prophecy said we would have to find a mountain that stood out from the rest, whatever that meant.

We continued trudging through the huge mountain range, fighting a few stray packs of monsters and easily dispatching them. We reached many different sizes and shapes of mountains, but none of them really stood out to any of us.

Rune, a Terra, said she would know if a mountain was different.

"Valen, could you fly us all instead of walking?" I asked, my legs starting to turn to jelly.

"I could," he said with a slight Italian accent. "But it would mean me passing out within the first fifteen, maybe twenty minutes."

"Dang it."

We walked in silence for another hour, and then I really needed to take a break. "Let's take a break for now," I sat on the ground, catching my breath.

The mountain range was slowly sloping upwards now, and it made it harder. Ashen coughed into his fist, not even out of breath. I shot him a look.

Valen was looking better than me, but still a little tired.

Nova was very out of her element (water) and she was probably the most tired of us all. She was trying to hide it, but it was kinda obvious. I smiled slightly behind my fist as she conjured some cold nice water to drink. I took out my water bottle and looked at the warm, old water in the bottle.

Reluctantly, I turned my head towards Nova. Valen, Rune and Ashen did the same. She was enjoying her sandwich. Rune cleared her throat. Nova looked up to find all four of us looking at her. She groaned.

"You guys just couldn't be all Aquas?" I gritted my teeth. "Ugh fine," she exhaled, frustrated.

We poured out the water. She closed her eyes and concentrated and all of our water bottles filled up with cold, refreshing water. We all drank and sighed.

Nova shook her head, probably not even realizing how good the water was. See? Annoying. We continued on with our journey.

"Guys," Rune said. We looked at her. "I feel something. Something big."

We started to get a little excited.

"I think it's the mountain we're looking for. We just need to walk maybe twenty more minutes."

I couldn't wait so I asked Valen to fly us one by one in the direction we were going.

Rune went first, after I comforted her. She was really really terrified of heights and wind. Ashen went next and he did it with no problem. Nova went after. She looked a little green.

"Don't be a wimp."

She stuck her tongue out at me and told Valen she was ready. She may or may not have screamed on the way there.

I went last.

"Are you ready?" Valen asked. I nodded slightly and braced myself. We took off. I trusted Valen, probably the most on the team (other than myself, obviously), so I knew I was in good hands. Also I wasn't afraid of anything. I was even called fearless.

We floated maybe fifty-something feet up in the air and shot towards my fellow questers in the distance. I screamed, but not out of fear, but joy and exhilaration. I landed softly, and a second later Valen landed right beside me.

He swayed and nearly fainted but Rune caught him. He smiled his thanks at Rune and she smiled back. They held each other's gaze for a moment too long, and then looked away quickly, both of them flushing red.

Ashen looked at me and raised an eyebrow. I shrugged and we headed towards the mountain Rune had felt. We reached the mountain and started to climb up to the part that Rune had sensed felt more magical.

"Stop," Rune said in a whisper. We all stopped walking. "Right here."

She pointed to a piece of the mountain that looked the same to the rest of us.

"So what do we do now?" Ashen inquired.

We all thought of different plans, none of them good. I came to the answer after Valen and Nova were arguing about creating an explosion.

"We need to use our powers. If the prophecy wanted us to come here, then it also knew that one person from each tribe would come as well. We all have to use our powers."

They all thought about it for a bit, and then looked at me grudgingly, knowing that was the answer.

Ashen started with a column of fire over his hand, after Nova summoned a floating ball of water. Valen called on the winds, as Rune closed her eyes and put her hand on the mountain. I closed my eyes as well and reached out towards the mountain with my mind.

"On three," I whispered. I didn't see their response, as my eyes were closed.

"Three."

Ashen and Nova held their hands closer to the mountain, nearly touching it.

"Two."

Valen had the winds circling around us.

"One."

In the space of a second, Ashen and Nova sent water and fire into the mountain. Valen forced the winds to obey, and Rune concentrated, her eyebrows furrowed together. I spoke in my mind towards the mountain.

OPEN.

A magical tunnel grinded open as I opened my eyes to the sight of my frien- sorry, teammates, all looking pale. That must've taken a lot out of them, but it worked.

We did it.

"I think that was a test," Valen remarked. "Maybe to get us to work together and to see if we were strong enough."

We all nodded at that and set off through the tunnel. It was not that wide of a tunnel, so we had to go two by two. Ashen was in the front. Me and Nova second, and Rune and Valen last. We walked in silence towards the light at the end of the tunnel.

We walked for what felt like forever and ever, and we really seemed to not be getting anywhere.

"Rune?" I said in a low tone.

"Yeah?"

"Are we getting anywhere? Can you feel anything?"

"Hmmm, it feels like something is blocking my sense of the earth. I can't feel anything."

I nodded and continued walking.

We were all getting bored and exhausted when the world shifted. My vision spun as we stepped out of the tunnel, through some kind of magical barrier. I looked back and saw nothing.

We were out of the border mountains.

We stopped to take a break, all of us exhausted. We drank our water and sipped some unicorn draught, which was like superwater that recharges you and gives you energy.

We rested for fifteen, maybe twenty minutes, and we were all feeling better.

That's when I heard the voice.

Robyn, the voice called in a soothing tone.

I looked around, confused, as my friends were gone.

Robyn, your destiny calls you. You must listen to me. I am your friend. The others are your enemies.

I started to feel myself slowly succumb to the soothing tone of the voice.

The voice could never hurt me. It was my friend. I shook my head, trying to get these thoughts out of my head.

I was Robyn Audo. No stupid voice was going to control me.

But... No. But the voice could-

No. No please.

I fell to the ground literally wrestling with myself.

It's ok Robyn. I understand. But if you listen to me, you

can have what you've always wanted. To be part of your kingdom. To have your family back. To just be accepted. Think about it, and when you call on me, I will be there.

A tear slid from my eye as I thought about my mom's beautiful smile as she cared for me all those years. About my dad's carefree and happy grin as we would have fun together.

All I wanted was to have a family again and be accepted.

I smiled. Could I finally be accepted and be reunited with my family? I decided that I would call on this voice the next time I had a problem, or a decision to make. What could go wrong? The voice was my friend.

I blinked and as I opened my eyes, I saw my friends eating their sandwiches and drinking water. I looked around to see if anyone had seen what happened, but they didn't seem to notice.

I smiled as I remembered the voice.

"We should get going."

My friends- no they were the enemies- but... No.

They all stood up and we continued north, towards the Tower of Secrets.

Soon, we encountered many stray monsters, but less and less as we entered the desert.

We were starting to get nervous as this desert was red. I think it was called the Desert of Red Sands. Red is the color of Chaos, so this seemed like a good place for monsters to be camping out. It felt weird that we didn't encounter any more monsters. It was on the absolute top of the map in the kingdom, past here, we would have no idea where we were going.

I guessed we would just have to continue north and hopefully find the Tower.

Like the mountain, the legend from the Aquas said we would know when we were there. Maybe Nova would sense some sort of special water magic or something like that.

❈❈❈

Ugh. Why did deserts have to be so hot? And humid. And sandy. And boring. My eyes were forever going to see red sand in small dunes. Not one thing wasn't red.

The sun was slowly setting, so the entire sky had a crimson/red tinge to it. We trudged across the red dunes until we saw them.

The monsters.

They had gathered and it seemed like word had spread that we had killed some of their brethren. There were hundreds of them, and they were all armed to the teeth. They radiated hatred and destruction as they snarled at us.

There were many different kinds, shapes, sizes, and colors of demons, but all of them had razor-sharp claws and fangs and were very, very angry.

Needless to say, I was excited. At last! We don't have to walk across the desert with limited water and sand getting everywhere.

I looked at my teammates and they readied their swords and bows. We were going to use our elemental powers, no doubt about that, but we weren't fully trained yet. It would tire us out before we could kill half of this army. That's why the best thing to do was to fight with a sword and with our powers, so they balance out.

We decided on a plan. Rune would raise a huge wall so we had height, but it wouldn't stay for long. Valen would do his best to scatter them with the winds and disorganize them. Nova would try and call water from the ground instead of conjuring it, because that would really drain her energy. She would flood the demons. Ashen would burn them, and I would try and control as many as I could, taking out the leaders first.

Nova wanted to just jump into the fray and fight. We said no, but I was wondering quietly if that would be a good plan as well.

We would all try and pick off as many as we could with our bows, but when the wall collapsed, we would have to charge in with our swords. It was a good plan, but we were all thinking the same thing:

Would it be enough?

Then we had no time to think, because the demons were charging.

We ran towards them, but at the last possible second, Rune pushed her hands up and we were riding a wall of dirt. We shot up maybe eight feet and then we stopped.

Valen spread his hands and the winds obeyed. Some of the demons were scattered, and some of them fell to the ground. Nova pulled water from the ground and sent in a wave towards the demons, and they barely moved. I guess they were fire demons or something. Maybe they were immune to water?

Ashen sent columns of fire through the enemy ranks, and threw fireball after fireball.

I controlled the General and he started to fight his own kind. I controlled the other leaders of the group, and soon it turned into demons fighting demons, demons sprawled on the ground, and demons getting microwaved.

I was running out of energy, and I think my friend-teammates were too.

We shot our bows at them, but their hides were very thick and had natural plates of armor. We realized that we would run out of arrows long before we pierced their hide.

The demons were just fazed from our attacks, maybe only fifty died.

They gathered ranks again, and took out their shields and slowly started to advance.

"We need to use our swords," Ashen remarked as yet another arrow bounced off the demon's shield.

"I don't know how much longer I can hold this wall," Rune admitted with a bead of sweat dripping down the side of her face.

I nodded and motioned for the rest of the team to pull out their swords. "On three, we jump off and kick some demon butt."

Everyone agreed, determination and fire in their eyes.

"Three."

The demons were getting closer. They seemed less scared of us now.

"Two."

We could smell them now, and let me tell you, they did not smell good.

"One."

We all jumped off the wall, screaming and yelling like maniacs, and the demons paused.

That was their downfall. We sliced and diced through the demons like paper. We were trained to fight, and fight we would.

I parried a demon's claw as Valen pushed all the demons back with the wind. He looked at me and I nodded. I slashed at a demon and stabbed at another. Nothing touched me as I slashed, parried, blocked, stabbed, and sliced through the rows and rows of demons.

Out of the corner of my eye, I saw Ashen encased in a ball of fire, nothing even coming close to Valen who was in a shield of air, rocks flying everywhere, and just chaos. The good kind.

We killed all the demons with our swords and elemental powers. We had a few scratches and nicks, and with some of the deeper cuts, we put on some bandages.

We all took a break and drank some unicorn draught. It was well into the night by then, around 10 PM. We decided we would continue to the Tower of Secrets tomorrow, because, first, we didn't have a map, second, we were all very tired, and lastly, it would be hard to miss a pitch-black tower that we didn't have directions to in the darkness, right?

Very easy. We set up the tent and the sleeping bags, and fell asleep.

❊❊❊

We woke up a bit later than before and set off towards the Tower of Secrets. The only thing good about more walking is the fact that we finally got out of that godforsaken, monster-infested desert.

Sorry if I have made deserts sound horrible. They are.

By noon that day, we had almost made it to the Tower.

We saw it around 11:30 and it looked... black. I know. Great description skills.

We were in a plain kind of area, so it was easy to spot the castle to our left. It was off to the side, and it almost looked like a pitstop. I wanted to go there but my friends didn't want to delay the quest any longer. I told them to wait one second.

I thought *Hey, uhh Mr. Voice? I need your help with this decision.*

The voice spoke in my head. *Good choice, to call on me. Like I said, I will always be there.*

I told the voice what the choice we had to make was.

I would suggest going to the castle. You never know, you might find something to help you on your quest.

I sighed in relief as the voice agreed with me. I turned to my friends, and told them I was going in.

They argued and pointed but I put my foot down. "We are going to that castle! If you guys are too much of wimps to go in, I'll go in myself."

I marched towards the castle. I reached the castle, and gasped.

It was much more magnificent than it looked from a distance.

My friends really didn't want to go in after Rune said, "I feel... something really powerful and a lot of magic. I don't think it's safe." The rest of my teammates agreed with her.

I shrugged and told them to wait outside. "I'll just go in for a few minutes and I'll come out," I said to them. I looked at the huge obsidian doors with the big designs on top, and I pulled on the door. The door was lighter than I thought, and I closed it behind me.

I looked around. The castle was glossy black obsidian webbed with gold. The floors were glossy black marble with big pillars. It was a hall. The welcome mat.

I walked past the many columns and pillars. There was another set of doors. I opened them. I walked into some sort of circular room with niches and glass containers. Each glass container held an artifact.

The first container held an amulet from Ancient Egypt made out of an unknown metal. The second, a lightning bolt that shone with power and buzzed like a horde of bees from Greek Mythology. The third held a huge hammer engraved with drawings and carvings from Norse Mythology, and in the fourth, a statue of an eagle from Roman Mythology.

But what really caught my eye was the artifact in the middle. It was a huge statue of an ancient dragon. It didn't look like a traditional Chinese Dragon, but something about it drew me closer. It looked like it was carved out of pure diamond. It looked very powerful, and when I looked closer, I could see the four elements circling around its body.

Wait.

No.

There were five!

Air was a current of wind, Fire was a blazing fireball, Water was a wave, and Earth was a boulder.

But there was one more. It looked like a spiral, but something about it made me think. That was my ability!

Now, I had the overwhelming desire to touch it. I grabbed a piece of cloth and wrapped it around my fist. I punched the glass and it shattered. The dragon glowed brighter as if it was expecting me. I could feel the heat and the power radiating from it as I reached out to touch it, but stopped.

What was I waiting for? The power and heat emanating from the statue of the dragon called me like a voice. I could nearly see my parents right in front of me smiling.

I reached out to touch it, and this time I did not stop. I touched the dragon with my palm. It started to hum and got warmer and warmer, and brighter and brighter, until it was so bright I couldn't look at it anymore.

Then it stopped. The dragon stopped humming and it went back to its original brightness and temperature. I cautiously approached the dragon.

Huh, I thought to myself. *It definitely sounded like it was building up its power for someth-*

My thought was cut short as the dragon exploded with the force of a bomb. I was thrown back so fast, I think my neck popped. I slammed against the hard black wall, and the last thing I remember myself saying was: "I think that might be bad," as well as small objects falling to the ground, before my vision spun and I passed out.

chapter 8
We Wake Up an Ancient Death Machine

It had been fifteen minutes since Robyn had entered the castle. Nova, Ashen, Valen, and Rune stood outside it, waiting for Robyn to return. With each passing minute, Nova became more weary. As she waited, Nova paced anxiously and thought about the danger Robyn faced.

"We need to go in," Nova finally said in a matter-of-fact manner.

"And why would we do that?" Ashen asked.

"You know very well why we would go in," Nova replied.

"We would go in because . . ." Ashen started.

"It's the right thing to do!" Nova finished.

"You're right. Let's go risk our necks for Robyn, the person who constantly controls us and forces us to do what they want," Ashen said. Ashen's response received soft snickers from Valen and Rune.

Nova looked directly at Valen and Rune. "Valen, Rune, shouldn't we help Robyn?"

"Yes," Valen and Rune replied quietly. Neither Valen nor Rune wanted to disagree with Nova.

"I don't think we should go in," Ashen persisted.

"Why not?" Nova asked.

"I told you! I don't like Robyn controlling me," Ashen said.

"I wonder who will betray us," Valen replied sarcastically.

"That's-," Ashen started.

An explosion jolted the castle, cutting off Ashen's response. Nova looked around at her four teammates frantically. Then she wasted no time and rushed into the castle. Valen, Rune, and Ashen followed close behind.

Inside the castle, the room looked like a bomb exploded.

Shattered glass laid across the floor and pillars previously lining the walls laid in crumbled heaps on the floor. Nova scanned the room for Robyn.

In her chaotic state, it took Nova a few moments of rushing around the room to find Robyn. Behind a pile of debris, Robyn laid back motionless. Nova frantically ran over to help Robyn.

"Robyn? Can you hear me?" Nova asked anxiously while nudging Robyn's arm.

Robyn remained unconscious. Nova looked around for anything that might help.

Water, Nova thought. Immediately, Nova conjured water particles from around the room to form a ball of ice cold water above her hand. Nova guided the ball until it hovered over Robyn's face. Slowly, Nova let go of the water. The ice cold ball of water splashed onto Robyn's face.

On the Other Side

"Gaaah," Robyn exclaimed after a few moments. Robyn looked at Nova and around the room in confusion.

Nova sighed in relief as she sat back.

Nova and Robyn looked at each other for several moments before Nova said, "Here drink this," and she put a flask of unicorn draught to Robyn's mouth. Robyn took a few gulps of unicorn draught before licking the liquid off their lips and slowly standing up.

"Thank you," Robyn said as they reached a hand down to help Nova up.

"Did you know you drool when you sleep?" Nova asked while smiling.

Robyn rolled their eyes and turned towards the crystal dragon who had apparently woken up.

chapter 9
We Nearly Become Supper

We all scuttled around and hid behind one of the obsidian pillars. We heard the dragon pacing back and forth, its feet echoing through the circular chamber. I remembered hearing the sound of things falling before I passed out. I peeked out from behind the pillar. Nova pulled me back.

"What are you doing?" she exclaimed in a harsh whisper.

"I heard something," I whispered back.

She released her grip from my shirt.

I looked around the corner again, seeing something I had not before.

First, there was the dragon, which I had seen, but what I noticed was behind it. Just under the glass cases, were indents in the wall, like something had been embedded there before. Long and pointed at each end, their glow slowly fading were four gems, one for each space.

Blue, red, clear, and green.

Their colour was still visible but like a central ember in the middle, seemed to be flickering and fading. Then they steadied at a dim glow.

Those must have been what had fallen when I had grabbed at the vision. But something was missing. I thought it showed 5 elements...

I looked around the room. Ahh there.

On the other side of the chamber, directly across from the others was a fifth gem and indent. A slightly larger purple gem. The Mind Gem. *My* gem.

I pulled myself back behind the pillar when the dragon sunk its steely eyes into me.

The dragon roared. Wait, do dragons roar? I think so... no, yeah, they do. Do they? Well the dragon made a very, very angry...? Well it screeched so loud that in the middle of it I may have asked Rune, who was next to me, if she could see blood coming from my ears.

"I think it saw me," I said in a small voice.

"I *told* you." Nova said to me. Obviously not too pleased.

"I know," I thought of a good way to retort. "And did I listen, no, what are you gonna do about it?"

She was planning on saying something but then I heard a raking sound. Like nails on a chalkboard. Followed by the sound of impact, stone on stone.

I looked up, the pillar was crumbling. Splitting horizontally just above the middle.

It came crashing down.

Ashen, Valen and Rune scrambled to the left and I pulled Nova to the other side. We tumbled right. I heard the dragon sneer over to my left. I opened my squinted eyes, and noticed that Nova and I were very, *very* close. I was silent for a second, before I found the right words.

"I- uh... The, um, others." See, told ya.

"Right," she responded. "But, what are those?" She gestured towards the 4 gems.

"I don't know, but they fell from their spots in the wall when I touched the dragon. In hindsight, maybe not the best plan."

She looked at me like *duh*, then waited for me to continue.

"I don't know their correspondence to the objects in the cases but, they seemed to be linked to the spell surrounding the dragon," I explained the floating visions around the once statue and the five elements circling it that I saw.

"*That's* what you grabbed?" was her response. I ignored it.

"I think they each represent an element. See?" I gestured at the different colours and then pointed across the room to the other.

Before she or I could follow up, my gaze drifted upwards towards the hot wet air blowing on my hair. I craned my neck and ended up looking straight up the snout of a gold dragon.

Uh oh, I thought.

We rolled over each other and out of the way just in time before the dragon bit down in our previous place. We shuffled and crawled under the fallen pillar, it was tight but we're both pretty thin, so we made it.

We extracted ourselves from the obsidian debris and

found ourselves locked in combat. The dragon was so large it took up most of the room. Before, on the pedestal, it was on its hind legs, wings folded, so it didn't take too much space. It was a large room but now the dragon felt larger.

I was grateful to spot the others relatively unscathed and blast the beast with every form of magic their element could take. Nova and I joined in.

"Shh, I have an idea," I whispered.

"Hey over here shiny!" Nova yelled.

I was starting to admire her defiance. She reminded me of me.

The dragon turned, making eye contact with both of us simultaneously. One eye on each of us. I seemed to wither under its gaze.

Nova was first to break from the trance. She blasted the dragon with a column of water. Like she popped the lid on a fire hydrant. She'd gotten really powerful since our last battle. She said something about how her magic is highly directional and *flow*, not force. I don't know.

The dragon snorted the water from its nose, but other than that the dragon seemed rather unfazed, just preoccupied. Like it was searching for an exit.

How long had that thing been frozen here? It must have been a long time based on the look in its eyes. It was a ruthless killer.

I thought.

We were all engaged in battle, but still tired from our last near fatal encounter. I thought I was scared then, gee, was I wrong.

"Nova, cover me." I said,

She stood her ground in front of me fending off the dragon whenever it turned our way.

I focused all my energy on getting inside its head. But it's armor was impenetrable. I tried to sense emotion. Nothing. Just that of the others around me, which were all relatively the same.

Panic. Panic and Fighting. Which wasn't an emotion, but I felt power surging, waves, earthquakes. All that drama.

I just couldn't break through the dragon's head. I knew nothing about this dragon. Persuasion wouldn't help me here. I knew what I had to do.

I found a secluded corner and called on the voice.

The voice spoke to me in a mellow tone.

Ah, finally. Do you need my help?

Well duh, I responded. *How do we defeat that thing?* I spoke in my head.

Oh, no. That thing can't be defeated. You must bind it. How did it break free in the first place? it questioned.

Well, that's kinda my fault. I touched the spell, I explained.

You fool! You're lucky I need you. I wanted to ask for what, but it seemed there were more pressing matters at hand.

Well I can't go un-break it! Tell me what to do!

Alright. Calm down, the voice soothed. *First each gem must be held by that of the proper tribe. Once you have sorted that out, you all must channel your magic through the stones. They are elemental gifts, do not, I repeat do not keep them, for then the spell won't work. I doubt any of you could deal with that,* it said harshly. *Then you shall use this new found power to force the crystal dragon back atop its pedestal. After-*

I cut them off. *Wait,* crystal *dragon?* I was confused.

Yes,

But it's gold...

Yes, will you let me continue or not? It asked annoyed.

I feel kind of bad calling you it. What would you like to be called?

I have no gender, they is fine. Same as you, I think we will get along quite nicely if you survive this. Now if you wish to... it paused.

Wish to what?

Survive.

What's new? We survived one day after another, yet it had gotten progressively harder as we went on. Is that what questing was?

Now whence the dragon is atop its altar, you will speak these words;

"Bonded again, the fate the Crystal Dragon befalls.

Stay and cause no more harm.

Don't resist for if you do,

We will curse you mercilessly.

Be warned"

Then perform the incantation.

What is the incantation?! I yelled silently because I could hear the voice fading.

And in a soft, sort of sleepy monotone, I heard: *Don't worry. I will guide you.*

"Guys!" my voice broke the sound barrier for the first time. For some reason when the voice spoke, my surroundings numbed until it was just me, and them. "It 's not going to work!"

"I realized that, but what else do we do? Let it eat us?" Ashen proclaimed that wonderful idea.

"NO!" we yelled in frustrated unison.

"Grab your power gem!" I yelled over the dragon's roars.

"Power what? Gem where?" Rune asked in a strained voice as she raised a chunk of debris. Funnily enough, my teammates had done more damage to the room than the dragon.

"There are five gems. Grab the one that matches your tribe colour!"

I didn't have a tribe colour, but I assumed the purple one was mine.

Not yours to keep, echoed the voice.

Then the dragon cooked us.

I don't fancy being microwaved. So, I dove behind a pillar and pressed my back against the cold stone. The dragon blasted around us, following the shape of the room. I prayed to whatever god I could think of that my friends were OK.

They're not your friends, the voice reminded me.

The fire curved around the pillar behind me, singing my arm hairs. The heat was so intense that it felt like it was pulling apart my molecules, and then dissolving them in lava.

Then it stopped.

My head ached, I slid slowly down the pole until I felt the floor. From my pack I sipped some unicorn drought, hoping to stop the burns.

I tiptoed around the outermost wall, trying to spot my... comrades. I saw Valen and Rune safely behind pillars, like me. I wasn't too worried about Ashen because he was an ember, hopefully this fire he could withstand. But then again I wasn't too optimistic either.

I found Nova crouched on the floor next to the fallen pillar. She seemed alright, just shaken.

I asked her, "Where's Ashen?"

Nova pointed a shaky finger to the wall opposite us. He seemed alright except for a few minor burns and scuffs. I doubt even a full fledged fire master could withstand that heat.

He had locked eyes with the dragon, clutching his sword in one hand and the gem in the other.

"Ashen," I snapped. "What do you think you're doing?"

"You said, 'get the gem'. So I did. The power, I feel it surging," Ashen spoke with admiration. "What do we do with them?"

He glanced nervously in Runes' direction, who was now making her way around to us.

"Everyone, I think we have to rebind the dragon. A spell was cast over this beast long ago because it is dangerous. We can't let it get free," I spoke, but doubt started to form in my mind. Could we actually do this? Were we powerful enough with the gems?

I tightened my grip on the purple stone and asked "Does everyone have theirs?" I lifted mine to show what I was talking about. "Here's the plan."

"A plan? What do you know that we don't?" Rune asked.

The voice responded in my head. *A lot actually.*

I sighed. "Do you want to die or not? Because those are our only two options. Unless you want to test our chances running from it?"

No one retorted.

"Alright, here's the plan." I told them what we had to do. "Fan out, make an even circle around the dragon, use your crystals and force it back atop its pedestal. I think you should be able to use the crystal to channel your magic through it. On three."

We all found our own space behind a pillar.

"One," I said.

We all readied ourselves.

"Two," I said.

Fear slowly creeped up into my throat, so I was stunned I got the last word out without bolting immediately afterwards.

"Three," we said in unison.

We jumped out from our hiding places. I held out my gem and the others followed suit. I gripped it so tight it cut the webbing of my thumb, but I didn't let go.

As soon as the others tried to use their magic it came out like a beam of coloured energy from their gems. Mine did the same. A lightning bolt of purple magic blasting like a solar ray.

I could feel the thoughts of the dragon, something I'd never done before. It wanted to be free. It had been stuck for a very long time. It just wanted out.

I almost felt sorry for the beast but then again, it *had* almost killed me.

I felt a high pitch ringing in my ears, so loud I almost doubled over, but I held my ground. I felt sorrow in the dragon, hurt, and anger.

The pain was almost unbearable now. For sure my ears were bleeding this time.

While the others moved it closer, pushing the dragon back, it took one step on the pedestal, I commanded it to steady itself atop it. I thought of those images of my parents. I thought of all the times I had been discriminated against, I thought of the pain and suffering I'd endured and focused all of that on the dragon, like it was their fault.

YOU WILL OBEY!

We forced the dragon into the center of the pedestal.

"What now?!" Rune yelled over the noise. The sound the magic beams gave off was like something being overcharged. Like a bunch of cicadas humming, really loud

In answer to her question I began speaking the words the voice told me to. I spoke to them with power and with reverence and the dragon seemed to shrink under me.

"Bonded again, the fate the Crystal Dragon befalls.
Stay and cause no more harm.
Don't resist for if you do,
We will curse you mercilessly.
Be warned."

Then I began to chant.

I have no idea where the words came from. I have no recollection of what they said, but they seemed to double the power from our gems.

Nova's eyes were wide open and she was smiling maniacally. She seemed to like the power.

The dragon twitched and writhed under the words. A thick mist swirled the dragon and formed different elements. Foggy shapes floating around them. Our gems tripled in power. I felt so good.

That was the only way I knew how to put it.

When I finished chanting I saw that the others were all staring. The power from the gems subsided to a low hum.

Put them back in their rightful place.

"Put them back," I said.

The others began to question but then we saw it.

The dragon started to move again.

"Put them back!" I yelled.

Once they were in their place, they glowed with powerful light. Illuminating the objects in the cases above. But mine did something different. When I stuck it in its place I heard a nice click. Like magnets attracting each other.

Then it blasted a beam of light at the dragon. I could feel the room vibrate with energy. The gold on the dragon dissolved, revealing a crystal layer of scales below. The coat shimmered with the different colours of the gems. The *Crystal Dragon.*

When my gem stopped the room spun.

It spun for about five seconds, knocking all of us off our feet. And when it stopped the room was in perfect condition. The burn marks were gone. The chunks of the wall Rune had been using to throw at the dragon had been filled, and the fallen pillar had been restored. The room was free of debris.

It really was quite a feat.

We walked out of the castle in a daze. From my vantage

point I couldn't see if the water gem was still in its place. I assumed so, I could trust Nova.

When we exited the castle, Valen was the first to break the silence.

"How did you know that spell?" Valen asked. "How did you know what to do?"

"I don't know," I lied. "The words just sort of... came to me."

He wanted to prod me further, so did the others, but we were all tired so for all our sakes, they- *we*, dropped it. We were so exhausted we just collapsed outside the castle. It's obsidian walls melting into the starry sky.

We made our way to the Tower of Secrets after taking a short rest.

Finally! We took 3 days just to start our quest.

We ate some food and drank unicorn draught and started off towards the Tower, where we would hopefully get some guidance from the ancient magician. We walked the last few metres and about a half hour later, we got a good look at the tower, and I had to say, it was pretty impressive.

The Tower was a large black structure with a huge glowing gate around it. It had mostly the same design as the castle, with veins of gold webbed through the huge obsidian blocks. The gates shone with protection spells. We walked up to the gates and they opened. The group looked at me questioningly. I shrugged and we walked through and looked up at the huge tower.

Chapter 10
I Hate Tests

"Finally, we're here," Ashen huffed.

"Oh, come on, isn't the air just amazing up here?" Valen replied to his pessimism.

"And the view." Rune stared in the opposite direction of the tower.

"Yes, yes it's all great but we need to figure out a way in." I tried to get the group together.

There was a massive chestnut brown door. I couldn't get over just how big it was. There was no door knob, only a rusty bronze knocker.

"Well, if no one else will knock I guess I will." Nova headed towards the door.

Compared to her, it looked like a skyscraper like the kind no-magics have in their cities. She clutched the knocker and took a deep breath. It was almost as if she was nervous but then again we all were at that point.

Thud thud!

It made a loud, low noise but nothing happened. The door stayed as shut as it ever had been and no one seemed to be coming to open it.

We all looked around. Over the cliff, around the trees and bushes, but nothing.

Suddenly a man stood right outside the door. He looked quite old. Almost in his seventies. Maybe late sixties. The point is, he didn't look like he aged well.

He stood there in silence while we all stared at him.

"Hello?" Valen questioned, just to make sure he wasn't dead or a statue.

The man replied with:

"If venturing further is what you seek,
You must reveal you are not weak.
To enter into the tower,
You will have but one hour.
Though this pile of stones be large,
You must build a structure as big as a barge.
While this seems easy you may flop,
for the largest stone must sit atop."

Then he disappeared again.

"Well, what does that mean?" Valen said again, still not sure if that man was real or not.

"Obviously, it's a riddle." Ashen mumbled, clearly still upset about Valen calling him a pessimist.

"Does anyone know what a barge is?" Rune questioned.

"It's like a huge boat," Nova answered.

"Thanks."

"Ok so it seems like we have to build a huge thing out of stones," I started. "It also says that the biggest has to be at the top which may be a minor inconvenience."

"Minor? No, that's way more than a minor inconvenience. Physics wouldn't allow it." Rune seemed like she thought this would be impossible.

"Well, lucky for us, we have magic."

"Thanks Valen. Way to state the obvious," Nova stated, sarcastically.

And just like that, everyone tried their own thing. Valen started pushing rocks on top of each other with air. He almost got it too, however the last rock, the biggest rock, made the whole tower collapse.

Rune tried to use things around her to help build the tower like trees and sticks. Once again the final stone made everything fall.

Nova tried making the water from a nearby stream pick up and place the stones. That didn't really do much but it was still a good effort.

Ashen tried picking up the stones with his hands but had to stop after only seven stones because they got too tall for him, (each stone was a little more than nine and a half inches).

Finally, it was my turn. I didn't know what my powers could possibly do to stack stones. Ashen's idea might have worked for me but I didn't consider myself to be very strong. I decided to go out on a limb and try controlling the stones with my mind. Not surprising at all, it didn't work.

Everyone started explaining why their idea was the best and eventually it turned into a full blown argument.

"Everyone stop yelling!" I yelled.

I guess yelling "don't yell" maybe sent the wrong message but everyone did stop so I guess it worked.

"I was going over the riddle in my head and I realized we all need to work together." I paused for emphasis. "We need to trust each other."

"OK Robyn, but um what's your plan?" Rune questioned what I was saying, just a little.

"So, I think that the best way to do this is Rune, you plant a tree right next to where the tower will be so it is supported. Nova you mix dirt and water to form a sticky paste that might help hold the stones together. Ashen you stack the stones until it gets too high for you, making sure there is Nova's paste in between each stone. Then, Valen will fly you up to continue the stacking. When it gets to the last stone, Valen will fly up with the whole rest of the paste, wait until it's a little dry then very carefully place the last stone. If we can all work together I'm sure this will work."

"Yes Robyn!" everyone said in unison. We all laughed about it before getting to work.

Just as I had planned, Nova was busy mixing the paste while Rune started growing a big tree. Ashen was busy stretching, very dramatically I might add, while Valen was resting because he had quite a bit of flying to do.

Once the paste was done, Ashen placed the first stone and Nova spread some paste onto it. Once Ashen and Nova couldn't reach anymore, Valen flew with Ashen, and Nova gave the paste to Rune, who climbed up the tree to add the rest of the paste.

The time came for the last stone. We only had about two minutes before the hour was up. Nova, Rune, Ashen, and I all stood to the side watching Valen with the last stone in his hands. Everyone was nervous. Valen took a deep breath.

One minute left. He placed the stone.

Thirty seconds left. The tower was sturdy.

Of course, we cheered and celebrated again. We headed back towards the door when the old man appeared again.

"You may not enter."

"But we solved the riddle!" Valen was defensive.

"That may be so but I will not allow any magical objects into my tower."

Nova had an uneasy expression on her face. She shoved her hand into her pocket as if she was trying to protect something.

"Nova! What did you do!" Ashen yelled.

"Nothing! I did nothing!" Now Nova was the defensive one.

"What's in your pocket!" Rune yelled.

"Nothing!"

"Nova you have three seconds to show us before I push you off the cliff. TRAITOR!" Valen had maybe gone a little too far. He outstretched his hands and started counting.

"No. Please no."

"Three!"

I didn't do anything, please no."

"Two!"

"Valen, don't you think you're going a little too hard

on her?" I tried to help.

"We all worked very hard to solve that riddle and now she's the reason we are going to fail?!?!"

Ashen snuck up behind Nova and quickly grabbed the thing from her pocket. "You kept the stone Nova!"

"Why Nov, why'd you do it?" Rune asked.

"I just thought maybe since we all became more powerful with it, that maybe I could keep it and stay powerful. Just maybe I wanted to be useful too!" Nova started crying a little now.

"You know we have to return that now." I told her.

"Yeah I guess." Nova looked disappointed, but knew it was the right thing to do.

Ashen handed Nova the stone.

"Will someone please go with me?" Nova asked.

Chapter 11
We Don't Put it Back and I Dodge a Question

"I'll go."

Robyn's volunteering to venture back to the cavern with Nova surprised some. Others gave them wary looks, perhaps insinuating that Nova and Robyn were *both* traitors. That was probably as far from the truth as humanly possible. Robyn didn't agree to go with Nova to put back the stone because they were somehow her evil accomplice, they did it because no one else would.

They couldn't help but feel sorry. So they went.

"Oh, and Nova? How about you *actually* put it back this time?" Valen sneered as Nova and Robyn turned to leave.

Robyn turned around on their heels. "She's going to. Right, Nova?" Robyn said, side-eyeing her.

Nova nodded a little too frantically, drying off the few tears that had escaped from her eyes.

Nova and Robyn set off down the path once again.

The first few minutes they both said nothing. Robyn wasn't exactly thrilled Nova had kept her stone, but she was Robyn's friend. They weren't about to make her go alone. That wouldn't be right.

"Why'd you do it?" Robyn finally asked.

"I-I just thought it would be good to have. You saw what it could do."

"I guess."

"Are you mad?"

"Not really, no."

"Oh, that's a relief."

"Why?"

"I don't want you to be mad at me."

They resumed their silence as they approached the castle, which was only about fifty feet from where they stood.

"I don't like dragons," Robyn said, wincing at the current memory. "I don't like the idea of going back there."

"It's alright," Nova reminded them. Robyn nodded with an exhale and they forged on.

"So, you and Ashen?" Nova said.

Robyn cocked a brow and turned her head. "Me and Ashen *what*?"

"I saw the way you two looked at eachother," Nova said, looking somewhat disappointed. Robyn wondered about this.

"Ashen is annoying most of the time. I don't like him at all," Robyn chuckled.

"You're lying."

"I don't lie much. I'm not very good at it. Besides, I like someone else."

"Who is it?" Nova questioned further.

"It's- Oh my God. Nova?" Robyn peeped. They'd paled at what they had seen.

As they forged further into the castle, the space became quieter. Darker. In the centre of the ominously quiet room, surrounded by four crystals was... nothing.

Nova suddenly appeared beside Robyn. "Robyn? W-where's the dragon?" she said quietly.

"It seems the dragon has escaped," Robyn replied. "We've gotta go tell the others."

As Robyn turned to leave, they noticed that Nova had gone in the other direction, deeper into the castle. As they pivoted, they saw that Nova was collecting the rest of the stones on the ground, slipping each colourful gem into the pockets of her parka.

"What are you doing?" Robyn cried. "We have to go!"

Nova exhaled. "I've decided to keep them."

"Why?!"

"Because they'll help us! I know it!"

Robyn hesitated, emitting a frustrated groan. "Fine. Just hurry!"

Robyn and Nova ran. Fast. They emerged from the castle still running, not hesitating for a moment.

"You never did tell me who you like!" Nova said as she ran, panting.

"Not the time!" Robyn responded, a blush creeping up their neck.

As they ran off as fast and as far from the cavern as

they could go, Robyn and Nova were determined to get back to the others.

Robyn just prayed that no one would find out that Nova carried four fold of the stone she promised she'd put back.

chapter 12
Tea Time With The Wizard Who Speaks Nonsense

The wizard led Ashen, Rune, and Valen in the direction of his tower. To get there, they had to walk through a somber forest. After a few minutes of walking, the wizard's tower came into their view.

The tower looked quite different without the protection spells on it. It was a tall, black, stone structure with moss and vines running up the side of it. It had a pointy roof and a couple of windows near the top.

The wizard opened the tall gate that surrounded his property. As they walked closer to the building, they noticed that there were a lot of birdhouses that the wizard had hung on trees. Not only were there birdhouses, but there also seemed to be other things hung on the trees. There were tin cans that were attached to strings tied up on tree branches as if the wizard was trying to create his own windchimes. There was also an odd number of garden gnomes beside the door that led into the tower.

The whole place seemed quite peculiar.

"Here we are," proclaimed the wizard. He adjusted his deep-red wizard robe and unlocked the door. "If you could follow me up the stairs please," he said.

They took a step inside and immediately noticed the tall spiral staircase. The wizard began to ascend the stairs and gestured for the others to follow.

As they walked up the long staircase, they noticed many strange drawings and paintings mounted on the wall. One painting, in particular, had caught Valen's eye.

It looked to be an old painting, as the colors were dull and the canvas was slightly torn in places. The painting on the canvas was quite unusual; it appeared to show a girl riding a dragon through the air. As Valen looked closer at the artwork he noticed that there was another girl on the dragon's back, she appeared to be asleep, or maybe even unconscious.

There were other peculiar paintings placed around as well. One thing that Ashen noticed seemed to be a drawing of what looked like an elephant with a dog's head. Rune noticed a small tapestry that displayed a series of interesting patterns. They all observed the many pieces of artwork as they followed the wizard up the staircase. What a peculiar collection of art!

When they reached the top of the stairs and walked into a room, they immediately noticed that there were even stranger pictures than the ones that were in the stairwell. Not only pictures but objects as well. There were various small artifacts placed around the room. Pottery, statues, jewelry, stone tools, even clothing. Though all of these objects seemed a little bit odd.

In the middle of the room, there was a small table with four seats. *Why would there be four chairs if he lives alone?* Ashen thought.

"Please, take a seat," said the wizard.

The three took a seat and noticed a small kitchen located in the corner of the room.

"I'll make some tea!" The wizard told them. He rushed towards the kitchen and got out a kettle.

As the other two observed the many items placed around the room, Ashen focused his attention on the wizard, who was moving frantically about the kitchen as he prepared the tea. The wizard's eyes looked dazed. It was almost as if he wasn't quite present in the moment; his mind was elsewhere. His skin was pale and wrinkly, and his arms and legs were boney and looked frail.

As he proceeded to make the tea, he stroked his grey beard and muttered words underneath his breath. Ashen listened closely, but still couldn't quite make out what the wizard was saying, so he refocused his attention back on the objects in the room.

There were multiple small tables scattered around the room with various objects sitting on top of them. One table had a collection of small stone statues. Another had a medley of small rocks and crystals. In a corner of the room, there was a small bookshelf, which looked to have very old books in it. One table even displayed a shiny silver dagger. Just like in the stairwell, this room had paintings of strange things hung up on the wall. *I wonder why he keeps so many things?* Ashen wondered.

A minute later, the wizard brought the tea kettle to the table, along with some precious-looking teacups and saucers. Rune examined the tea set. The base color for the porcelain was light pastel pink, and the handles on the kettle and cups were a shiny bright gold. For the print on each cup, there were a few small gold flowers and one big one on the kettle. The saucers were the same pink color but instead of having flowers, the lip of the plate was painted gold.

"This is a lovely tea set," Rune acknowledged. "Where did you get it from?"

The wizard stared blankly at his teacup before saying anything. He reached out and began pouring the tea while muttering strange words, and shaking his head.

"The dragon... ride... save... her... love..."

It sounded like total nonsense.

The three looked at each other, all of them with confused expressions on their faces.

When the wizard finished pouring the tea, he asked, "Would any of you like milk or sugar?"

They all shook their heads.

"No thank you," said Valen. "We're here because you said if we passed the test, then you would provide us with the guidance we needed."

"And we passed the test," Rune continued. "So..."

The wizard began pacing back and forth, shaking his head and muttering, "No, no, no, no." He quickly turned around and looked Ashen in the eyes. "Where's your friend?"

"Oh, Nova?" Ashen replied.

"No, no, no, the other one."

"Robyn?"

"Yes!"

"I mean, we're not really friends…"

"Doesn't matter. Where are they?"

"Umm… well, clearly not here."

"That was helpful information," Rune rolled her eyes.

"Tell. Need to tell. Need to tell." The wizard went on and on muttering nonsense.

Valen and Rune gave each other a concerned look. The wizard sat down and tapped his fingers on the table. He picked up his teacup and took a sip.

Ashen looked at him. "Don't worry, Robyn will arrive soon."

The wizard's hand started shaking. Rune was worried that he'd drop the teacup (clearly this tea set was expensive). "There. Go. You will do. Go."

Suddenly the wizard put down his teacup, and the whole room went silent.

Chapter 13
I Am Told to Leave

Robyn and Nova arrived back to the tower breathless. They rushed inside and found Ashen, Rune, Valen, and the wizard drinking tea. They looked up at Robyn and Nova, who had faces of alarm.

"The dragon," Robyn starts. "It's gone."

✳✳✳

I looked around and everyone but Nova and the wizard were looking at me with expressions that screamed: "What?!"

They looked at Nova for confirmation of what I had just said, and she nodded.

The wizard was looking at me. He seemed to be confused, yet scared at the same time. He was blinking a lot and one of his fingers was twitching, causing his teacup to shake slightly.

Was he OK? Or...

He looked out one of the windows and into the distance. I turned my attention back to the four others and I saw them asking questions, frantically.

Everyone seemed to be in a panic, the wizard included, and I couldn't handle it.

CALM DOWN

Using everything in me, they did so. Everyone looked at me, but I was frozen.

Robyn, the more emotion you put into your orders, the more they work. And the most powerful emotion is anger. When you let it consume you you have more control. More power. You know that dont you? You want that dont you? Power.

The wizard's teacup fell to the ground and shattered into a million pieces. He turned away from the window and stared at me.

Creepy.

His blinking and twitching rate had gone up. Not that I was paying a whole lot of attention to it.

"Go," he spoke. It was barely a whisper, but everyone noticed.

Okay, how was it that when I spoke normally nobody heard me, but when he went and whispered everyone heard it?!

"Go," the man said louder. He pointed to the door shakily.

What was with him?

"Is this because of Robyn's gender?"

Everyone turned to see the wizard's reaction to Nova's accusation.

"Because if it is," she continued. "It doesn't change the person they are."

"No, it is not because of that. It is something else," he answered.

He looked at me again. It was really creepy. "Go," he repeated.

"But we haven't done anything, " Valen says.

"It's not what you have done, it is what you will do," the wizard said.

Gosh, he was so confusing. Was he scared about us saving the world? Did he not want us to save the world?

Rune looked at us. Ashen, Nova and Valen were equally confused as to why he wanted us to leave.

"Is he talking about the betrayal from the prophecy?"

I shrugged my shoulders, even though, when I really thought about it, I was fairly certain he was. Which would mean that he knew the prophecy, and how it would turn out. What else did he know?

Robyn, on the highest level of the tower, there is a great power waiting. If you really want your parents back, if you want to be an equal, to be normal, take it. Use it. And you will have everything, the voice spoke.

My parents.

Suddenly memories of the past flashed in my mind.

Walking down to the playground hand-in-hand with them. Me eating mint-chip ice cream and my father, chocolate (our favorites). My mother homeschooling me. Blowing out the candles of my tenth birthday. And having them read me to sleep when I was five.

I left the trance of memories and I noticed that the wizard looked at me when I did.

"Your friend I know. The outcome, no. Too much! Too much!" He started to freak out again, running his long pale fingers through his hair and grabbing it at the ends.

He must've really been mad.

But anyway. The voice had said something about how I could get my parents back.

❆❆❆

The wizard and the others were still sitting around the table. Ashen, Nova, Rune and Valen were talking about the riddle and the wizard was still staring off into the distance, white in the face and purple eyes wide.

If I was honest, he looked constipated.

As for me, I was going to the highest level of the tower.

chapter 14
I Climb an Endless Staircase

After about three steps, I looked up. It looked like there were literally four hundred and ninety-seven more steps. I continued marching.

Every so often there would be a very small landing where I would look through a frosted window and see the scene on the bottom floor of the tower. I saw everyone talking. Nova looked very troubled, but I thought nothing of it at first.

I got bored so I started counting how many steps were between each landing. Then, I wished I hadn't because one time it would be sixty-two and the next, forty-eight. Sometimes, it would be fifty-three while others would be forty-seven. All that counting was hard, but it did distract me from how long I was climbing for.

Finally, the last step! I never wanted to climb that many stairs again.

There was a small old chair up on the top floor of the

tower. I thought I deserved a break for I had just climbed five hundred stairs. I knew I couldn't take too long because as Scribe Fallon often reminded me, we had things to do and very little time to do them.

I looked out the big window and saw everyone talking again. But this time Valen, Ashen, and Rune looked very upset and Nova looked like she wanted to cry again. I didn't blame her, though. I would as well if I was being yelled at by three of my... um... friends?

I heard the voice again.

No! No! They are not and will never be your friends. Don't get distracted, let's see what's up here.

I looked around. According to Rune, this floor was made out of oak wood. The walls looked like they were about to crumble. This whole tower looked like it must be held up by magic.

Then I realized, it probably *was* held up by magic.

There were only four things in this room: the chair that I sat in, a small broken table, a very dusty rug that looked to be about a million years old, and a chest. The chest wasn't exactly new but it did look like it was maybe a hundred years newer than the rest of the old stuff. The only light came from the broken dirty windows (if it was daytime).

I headed towards the chest. It wasn't a far walk, considering the room was quite tiny.

The chest was locked and I couldn't see a key. I started to check around the room for a key.

The rug. Check under the rug. I did just that and sure enough, the key was there. If I was being honest, I really didn't want to touch that rug or the key, but when duty calls.

I inserted the key into the keyhole and turned it clockwise. The chest opened with a cloud of smoke (or dust). Inside was a piece of parchment that looked to be extremely old, along with the rest of the room.

I looked out the regular window to see Nova, walking away from everyone.

5 MINUTES EARLIER

The group walked outside to argue.

"Nova, you don't belong with us, you're obviously the traitor!" Ashen yelled, still not cooled off yet.

"You jeopardized this whole visit by keeping the stone. You betrayed us all, even Robyn," Rune stated.

Nova was upset by the mention of Robyn being betrayed.

The Wizard stepped inside to let them talk, or argue, alone.

"I'm sorry it was an accident. I didn't know it would affect anything," Nova frowned.

"Wouldn't affect anything?!?!" Valen started. "Yes, because a very important, powerful stone wouldn't affect anything. Sure."

"You need to go, Nova. We can fulfill part of the prophecy if we get rid of the traitor. We know it's you, now go away."

Ashen was really mad at Nova.

"Guys I'm really sorry. I wouldn't ever do something to intentionally harm you all. Ever."

"Don't try and make us feel sorry for you, we won't."

Valen and Ashen agreed.

"I don't know guys, maybe Nova did just make a mistake." Rune was starting to believe her.

"Don't fall into her trap, Rune." Ashen tried to keep her away from turning to Nova's side.

"Yeah Rune, she wants you to feel bad for her," Valen added.

"No, please listen to Rune. Trust me." Nova's voice lowered after she realized no one was going to help her.

Where was Robyn when she needed them?

Nova looked up to the top of the tower.

It was in the clouds but she still managed to look into the big broken window. Robyn was there walking towards something. They looked like they were talking to someone or something, but Robyn was alone up there (as far as anyone knew).

"What did we say, Nova? We need you to leave." Rune was convinced by Ashen and Valen to make sure she left.

"Okay fine, but just know that I actually did consider all of you my friends and I know that obviously, now you don't. But I hope that at least at some point, I wasn't just some dead weight, I was useful." And with that Nova walked off.

"Are you sure we made the right choice?" Valen asked, doubtful.

"Yes I'm very sure. She almost messed up the whole quest." Ashen had no doubt in his mind that Nova was the traitor.

"Yeah, I guess you're right Ashen." Valen and Rune were also sure about Nova.

On the Other Side

❊❊❊

I saw the scroll, but just as I was about to grab it, I looked at the seeing glass and saw Nova walking away. I quickly shut the chest and rushed downstairs.

No! What are you doing Robyn! Get the scroll! The voice was very mad.

"I need to go get Nova."

She is not your friend! None of them are.

"You're wrong! She is my friend and I will defend her."

Go back and take the scroll.

I didn't even consider going back because I did not want to go back up all those stairs.

I finally got all the way down.

"Where's Nova going?" I frantically asked the wizard.

"I don't know. I'm just busy here making tea," the wizard responded.

"Um okay. Thank you, anyway,"

Just as I was about to walk out the wizard continued. "Herbal tea."

"Um okay. You have fun with that." I flung the door open and desperately searched for Nova on the horizon "Where is she! Where's Nova?"

"We made her leave," Rune replied.

"Yeah, she ruined our quest so we sent her off," Valen stated.

"She is the traitor," Ashen commented.

Chapter 15
The Microwave Returns

I ran after the small figure in the distance after hearing this news, thinking I had to go after Nova, but Valen stopped me with the winds. I was running, but I wasn't moving forward. I growled.

"Let me go after her! She might be in danger!" I protested.

"Nope. We kicked her out, and what's done is done. You should be thanking us, she was the traitor of the prophecy," Ashen said.

"Come on! There's no way she's a traitor! She would never betray us!" I shouted at my so-called "friends".

"But she took the gem after you specifically told her not to," Valen said.

"Yeah, how do we know we can trust her? Huh?" Ashen said with a sneer on his face.

"Rune you believe me, right? Rune?" I said desperately, grasping at straws.

Rune looked sad, but she shook her head slowly. "I just don't know why she did that."

I exhaled, frustrated as Ashen, Valen, and Rune just turned their backs on someone we used to call our friend.

Maybe someone more than a frien- *cough*.

What did I say? Nothing. Yeah, I said nothing. No need to worry. But I just couldn't believe them as they sat back down like nothing happened.

"Please," I pleaded.

They shook their heads and sipped their tea. UGH!

"Nova will be out there all alone! We don't even know who or what's out there and you just kicked her out!" I lowered my voice, racked with emotion. A tear slid from my eye. "You've sentenced her to death..." I said quietly through tears.

I gritted my teeth and turned my back on them like they did to Nova. I walked up to the second floor, past the wizard, needing some time alone.

How could they even do something like that? I don't ev- even understand.

It's okay Robyn. I told you they were never on your team. They are the real enemies. You shouldn't listen to them. All they're trying to do is get into your head. Listen to me. Remember, I can help you get your family back. I can help you be accepted.

I felt the soothing voice in my head calm me down slowly. *But how could they?* I thought.

I don't know Robyn. I don't know why they sentenced Nova to death. I'm truly sorry.

And I knew the voice meant it. It felt like losing my

parents all over again. My sorrow and grief turned to anger and rage. I tamped down the emotions for now. I thought about it, and I could do something this time.

When I lost my parents all those years ago, I could do nothing. If my friends wouldn't save Nova, I would do it myself. I calmed down more until I was ready to face my teammates again.

I was about to walk down the stairs when I heard a huge roar, which was followed by the roof of the tower exploding into small pieces, being eaten by the huge crystal dragon.

The dragon was back for more.

The rubble fell down from the top of the roof and crashed down through the many, many floors. I dodged a bigger chunk of the ceiling as my 'comrades' screamed from below. I ran down the stairs.

The Wizard chuckled as he drank his tea from his small cup. His robes were covered in dust, as well as his face. He wiggled his fingers in a hello, apparently forgetting that I was scary, and I nodded. He noticed his broken teapot and broke into tears.

The tapestries, drawings and statues were ripped and some of them were destroyed. The wizard didn't notice and continued to cry over his teapot.

My friends were fully covered in white dust, and a huge chunk of the roof had crashed right onto the dining table. They were all sitting there in shock, eyes wide and jaws dropped. I was 95 percent sure Ashen had wet his pants. I suppressed a small smile.

Rune was the first to regain her senses, and moved

the rubble off the table. Valen blew the dust off the rest of us, with the winds, and Ashen excused himself to use the washroom. He went up the stairs before remembering that the dragon was still there.

He quickly ran back down the stairs. He was fixing his hair and trying to look normal. He tried to hide the big spot on his jeans but it was pretty obvious. We all smiled as he coughed unnaturally.

We rushed out the door to see the dragon on the broken roof, while the Wizard was still crying. "I'll be okay, don't worry about me!" He called to us through heaving sobs. I stepped back away from the huge crystal dragon and thought of something.

"Now might not be a good time, but Nova actually has all the stones…" I said sheepishly.

Ashen gritted his teeth. "And you couldn't let her go, huh?"

"Hey, we decided to take all of them together," I muttered. I turned my back on him.

Ashen coughed. "Yeah, she totally didn't smile at you and force you to listen to her."

I tensed and turned to face him. I shot him a glare. "Not the time Ashen!" I turned back towards the dragon, who was still on the roof.

He smiled, pleased that he was able to get under my skin.

I forced him to slap himself in the face. Hard. He winced in pain and it was my turn to smile.

He growled under his breath, "I'll get you back for that, don't worry."

"Try me," I smiled and stuck my tongue out at him.

He pounced at me, and Valen pushed us apart with the winds. He and Rune were on the verge of laughing.

"You guys can argue all you want later. Let's defeat this dragon first."

Ashen and I silently made a truce.

The dragon breathed fire and we scattered again. The raging-hot fire nearly engulfed us and we almost became microwaved, but luckily Ashen just barely deflected the blast to the side, cooking the sand into red glass.

"I really wish we had Nova for this fight," I commented pointedly towards Ashen.

He spread his hands. "Are you sure that you don't want her here for anything else? Maybe a kiss would be ni-"

He was cut off by his own hand, punching himself in the stomach repeatedly. Valen flicked his hands and we both fell to the ground. My concentration was broken and Ashen could stop punching himself. Stupid Auras.

Valen walked in between us. "Hey, we said we would discuss this later." He and Rune were having trouble suppressing their laughter now. I glared at him and Rune and they both instantly looked away. Ashen slowly stood up groaning, but he looked mostly okay.

The dragon roared as it apparently was ready for us. It spread its crystal wings wide and dived down towards us. At the last possible second, we scattered.

"Looks like we're fighting this again," Valen remarked.

"Yeah, but without a crucial member and our powerful gems. Hmm. I wonder who made that decision," I answered, glaring at Ashen.

He didn't even have the decency to look embarrassed.

"Whatever. We beat this dragon once. We can beat it again," he said, raising his sword. We all did the same and nodded to each other.

We charged towards the dragon, swords raised and powers ready, yelling in defiance.

※※※

The lone girl walked away slowly from the huge looming tower in the distance. She was saddened, but didn't understand how they could think she was the traitor.

Maybe I am the traitor, she thought sadly. She opened her bag and looked at the five different color gems. They really were beautiful. She picked all of them up and examined them.

She put them back in her bag, regretting her decision and wishing she had done the right thing. She trudged her way back into the desert and started back home through the mountains.

She stopped for a quick rest beside a small mountain with a cave. The girl opened her canteen and drank deeply, tears swelling in her eyes.

She took a long drink and thought about Robyn, her friend. Then she thought about the prophecy.

She was deep in thought, eating a sandwich and drinking some water when the hooded attacker struck. She yelled and summoned a wave of water, and smashed it into the attacker's face.

The attacker didn't even blink and punched the girl

in the face. She cried out in pain and kicked the attacker in the skin. The hooded person winced in pain and hopped on one foot, but recovered relatively quickly.

The attacker pulled something from his pockets. The girl shouted but the attacker sedated her with a needle. The girl thrashed but her movements were getting sluggish.

She fell unconscious and the attacker grabbed her by her arm and slung her over his shoulder. He walked away with the unconscious girl over his shoulder, pulling out his silver knife...

chapter 16
There's Nothing In My Bag, I Promise

"You're coming with me, don't say a word," the man said. He was dressed in all black and wore a mask so Nova couldn't identify who he was. He held a knife up to her throat and covered her mouth so she couldn't say a word.

Nova tried to pull away, but she knew that all that would do was make things worse. She mumbled, "Let me go," but it was no use, he wouldn't. He walked while dragging her for what seemed like hours, in reality it was probably thirty to forty five minutes.

Nova had no idea where he was taking her, but she knew it wouldn't be good. After all, what hostage situation turned out well?

Eventually, they reached a destination. Nova couldn't really see straight because it was extremely foggy but what she could make out was this dark and deep cave. The opening was quite small but the inside was enormous. The man took her to the end of the cave. Probably so that nobody could hear from the opening. He threw her to the ground, which hurt more than she expected.

"Ow, that hurt!" Nova said, panting.

"You know what could hurt more? This." He pulled the knife out.

"Okay, okay, what do you want? Please don't hurt me" she pleaded.

"I want what is in your bag."

"I don't have anything in my bag."

"Don't lie to me, if you don't give them, I will take them myself."

"I told you, I DON'T HAVE ANYTHING IN MY BAG!" Nova raised her voice which was a bad idea.

"Don't forget I am stronger than you. Don't raise your voice, because I can raise it much louder. I could tell Robyn what your parents did." Nova winced.

Anything but that. Robyn couldn't know that; it would ruin their relationship.

"Listen," Nova's voice lowered because even though she tried to act brave, she was terrified. He had a knife! "I don't have anything in my bag. Please," Nova begged. "Don't tell them."

"You have 3 seconds to take what is in your bag out, or I will. Don't test me little girl. Three."

Nova didn't budge.

"Two."

Nova didn't budge.

"One."

Nova's nerves got to her. She reached into her bag to feel the warmth of the five stones. She almost forgot that she had these in there.

She panicked. She couldn't just give this man the five most important stones that were probably the only way for them to complete the quest successfully. But if she didn't, he would slice her.

Nova thought on her feet. If she gave this man four stones and not five then he wouldn't be suspicious because she doubted he knew about the mind controlling one. She would give him the fire, water, earth, and air stones, and not the mind controlling one. She suspected that he wouldn't expect this stone because it was extremely rare and not many people even had heard about this power being a real thing. Without the four elemental power stones, things could turn out bad, but maybe because the mind controlling stone was more rare and dangerous, it could be more powerful. So maybe it could defeat more than they knew.

Nova looked into her pocket, quickly scrambled through the stones and got the white, red, green and blue stones, leaving the purple one tucked into its spot. She held them tightly in her palm and hesitantly handed them over.

The man instantly snatched them from her. He chuckled a little and took a nice look at the stones.

"This is exactly what I need," said the man.

He looked at the fire one first, then the earth, then the air. Lastly, he looked at the water one. He looked more closely into this stone than the others, which Nova thought was odd.

The man was too focused on the stones and seemed to have forgotten Nova was even there. He was so determined that his mask was not even fully covering his face, and Nova was able to take a glimpse of who it was. She recognized him instantly. It was her uncle and she knew exactly why he wanted the stones.

A long time ago, Nova's parents were very close with her uncle and so was Nova. He was like a second dad to her. He cared a lot about Nova and her parents. He would take care of Nova and play with her. But all of that changed when Nova's dad became vice head of the Aquas. That was something Nova's uncle had been talking about ever since he received his water powers. When Nova's dad got the opportunity and he didn't, Nova's uncle got jealous. He turned completely on her family and was always in competition. Since then, they had stayed away from each other and never spoke. When Nova's parents died in a car crash, it was almost like her uncle was glad because he knew that he could have a chance of being vice head. But that didn't happen, her dad's best friend got it.

Her uncle was there now, looking for these stones because he knew that taking them back to the head of the Aquas would get him some type of promotion. He would take them back and the head would be so proud of him. Because not only did he have the water stone which made the Aquas much more powerful, but he also had the fire, earth and air stones which could make those sectors weaker if you knew what to do.

Nova was ashamed of what she had done. She had given this man who had turned on her family the most powerful stones. She regretted taking them from the tower. "I should have listened to the others," she thought.

Soon after, the man noticed that Nova was looking

at him strangely so he rapidly slipped the stones into his pocket. Nova wasn't scared of him. Even though he practically hated her, he wouldn't kill her. The knife was just there to scare her.

"I know who you are, Uncle Dave." Nova stood.

He looked at Nova in shock.

"I'm not your uncle," he said.

"You're pretty bad at lying. Nothing's changed, I see," Nova responded. "You're still the same pathetic self who doesn't care about anyone but himself. You were so stubborn that you turned away from your family who loved you, who you once loved."

"You don't know anything," He screamed.

"I know all I need to know."

"And if you don't shut your mouth, I will tell your new boyfriend, Rob."

"They're just my friend!"

"Whatever, you wouldn't want them to know what your parents did to their parents, pretty much the cause of Robyn's parents death," he said.

He pulled his knife out.

This time, Nova wasn't scared. Realizing the knife didn't scare her, he put it away.

Instead he reached into his other pocket and pulled out a needle. When you had one of those injected in you, you'd be passed out for at least two hours.

Nova tried to run but slipped on the rocks and fell to the ground. He pulled off the cover and jabbed her neck before she was able to block him. He quickly put tape over her mouth and tied her to the edge of the cave. Nova couldn't move.

Myth and Magic Crew 10

All Nova saw was her uncle running with the stones and she couldn't even run after him. She fell into unconsciousness shortly after.

chapter 17
Fighting a Crystal Dragon is Very Hard

Fighting a crystal dragon was very hard, don't let anyone tell you otherwise. And what made the matter even more difficult, was the fact that I told them that Nova had taken all of the other gems when we had gone back to return the first one she took.

Seriously, everything was going wrong.

But back to the real point.

We were all trying to fight the dragon, who was probably trying to kill us, like we were doing to him.

Ashen was throwing massive fireballs at it, hoping to stop it, but failed miserably. It had barely done anything to stop the dragon. Rune and Valen were working together to make boulders fly and hit the dragon in the face.

At least they were working together! They seemed to really get along those two.

Everyone was trying to make the dragon fall, but nothing seemed to be working. The wizard had thrown a couple of potions at it, but its sharp scales seemed to deflect them.

Suddenly, Ashen's face lit up. Like as if a lightbulb had appeared above his head. Which was something you didn't see too often.

"Rune, I need a really tall tree," Ashen yelled to her.

Rune looked at him. What would he possibly need a tree for?

"Right under you?" she asked him.

"Yes, I need it to lift me up!" he screamed back.

She looked confused as to why he wanted a tree to grow under him, but obliged.

And soon, Ashen was at the top of the growing tree, going higher and higher into the air. Was he trying to get himself killed? Or was he just that stupid?

My guess was the latter.

"Hey dragon," he yelled. The dragon turned its whimsical eyes to look at Ashen, who was just as high at the dragon's face. "Take this!" And he shot fire into one of its eyes.

For the first time, the dragon rumbled loudly in pain.

Its.. hand? Went up and covered the eye that was hit. Its shiny crystal tail started whipping in every direction.

And I really should not have laughed, but it hit Ashen, making him go flying.

His screams echoed through the air and all his limbs were waving around. His face looked panicked.

Luckily, Valen was able to catch him with the wind before he touched the ground and died. When he got back up he looked as if his life had flashed before his eyes. His reddish hair was a mess and he was trembling. He clutched where the dragon's tail had hit him and fell back on the ground.

He was so overdramatic!

I mean, you were only hit in the stomach by a crystal dragon!

Then a thought came to me, could I control the dragon?

I thought about it for a second and decided to give it a try. I took a deep breath and screamed in my mind.

STOP!

It made my head hurt, but I kept screaming it in my mind, hoping that the dragon would follow orders. And when I opened my eyes I saw it had. It was standing there, motionless, looking down at me.

Now, get down onto the ground.

It reluctantly did. I sighed in relief and happiness. I looked over at the others and they bore surprised expressions.

It lay down its head at my feet and very silently let out a sort of breath. Then, it lifted its head, as if telling me to get onto its back.

I looked at the others.

"Sorry guys," I said, and I got on its back, trying to get in a comfortable position. They looked at me with sadder faces than anything I'd seen from them before. "We need Nova," I told them.

"But she took the gems, she betrayed us," Valen argued.

"She had good intentions, and even if she took them, I knew about it. And you guys didn't throw a fit over me." I let out an angry sigh. "Not that I'm complaining, I adore not being yelled at, for once. But we need her. And I have a feeling she needs us too. So if you guys won't go. I will." I finished my speech and looked down at the dragon.

Bring me to Nova, I commanded.

And the dragon slowly rose off the ground. Its long thin wings spread around us. I steadied my hands on its back so I wouldn't fall, and we flew off.

"I'll find you Nova."

chapter 18
I Have a Love Life?

I was high in the sky within seconds. It was hard to keep control at first, I had to focus all my energy on not falling off to the point that I could barely keep a good grasp on the dragon's mind. Eventually I got a hold of it and started in a direction. I flew west, the same direction I watched Nova leave in.

I missed her. I was scared for her. Listen, I cared so much more about Nova than I cared to admit. She was funny, charming, impulsive and... well, like me. Did that sound narcissistic? I didn't care.

Although I was focused, it was a difficult state to maintain. I had to balance the dragon's mind and control it while my subconscious looked for Nova.

Just before the tower left my line of sight, I saw them.

Was I being followed? By dragons?

They were heading south over the border mountains, back to our kingdom.

I saw smoke in the distance. The dragons passed right above the tower. Four of them, a blue and silver one, a green and gold one, a deep red and black one, and a pearly white one. From this distance I couldn't tell their size, but over the top of the broken tower they looked massive, with the same wing structure and body as the one I was riding.

Where were they going? Why go back that way? Was I supposed to follow? As I was distracted, I lost grip of the dragon and I fell.

Slipping sideways heading straight for the mountain range below, I was obviously screaming. I mean, who wouldn't? I lost all connection to the Crystal Dragon. I literally thought I was going to die.

The dragon dove after me, under me and stopped. I fell, landing on my belly, sliding and tumbling down to the tail. I tried to claw my way up, slowly slipping further. The dragon dipped its head and I rolled downward. I shuffled carefully so I was back on its back.

I held on tighter from then on.

I scouted the endless mountain range. I'll spare you the details. Mountain and sky. Cold. Cold wind, yeah.

As I soared through the air, miles above ground, I spotted a cave.

Hundreds of feet high inside an innermost valley I was flying through, was a thin steep mountain path, zigzagging up the cliff face. At the top was a dark opening. I landed on a near cliff edge to do some recon. Just cause mysterious caves in secluded areas where nothing was supposed to live, kinda gave me the feeling that I should be careful. Not that I had much experience with them.

I saw a light flickering from the inside. I flew down to the base and commanded the dragon to stay put. I doubted I had a rope either strong, or big enough to tie this guy up. I patted the dragon's snout and thanked it for saving me, for I had not done it before. The dragon gave me a confused look as it looked up at the cliff. I chuckled. Then I made my way to the start of the rocky uphill path.

Around halfway up the hill the path got really narrow. I walk with my back pressed against the mountain behind me. I stumbled and shimmied, scared, upward. I slipped. Stones rolled out from under my feet. I hit my chin on the edge of the outward niche as I clutched the side of the mountain. More rocks tumbled. My left hand came free of the edge.

"Agh! Help!" I screamed, though there was no one for miles. I lost grip with three fingers. I wasn't strong enough.

You have a dragon...

The voice reminded me.

Oh. My. Lord.

I cursed aloud. Things I won't repeat again in fear of getting my mouth washed out with soap.

Idiot! I scolded myself.

I called upon the dragon. He came within seconds. He? I think?

Gracefully, very gracefully, mind you, I slid down the cliffside and landed on the dragon's back, who took me the rest of the way.

He plopped me on the thin protruding edge in front of the cave. I sighed with relief. Had I even breathed since I fell? I didn't feel like it.

I looked inside and saw a flickering fire. *Whoosh.* The wind blew the fire out.

***

"Nova!" I cried as I released her from her bonds. "How? What?" I stammered but I couldn't form a full sentence. I was so relieved.

She tried to speak but was too weak. Then she passed out. Cold.

She was shivering fiercely. I wrapped her in a shawl I packed for some reason and dribbled some drought into her mouth. She was bonded far away from the fire. Nothing to keep her warm. But, she had water powers... So she should've been able to withstand this weather, for water was ice too. I touched her head. She was burning.

"What happened here?" I questioned aloud.

She was poisoned.

"Poisoned?!" I yelled, upset. I thought I was going to cry. "Is she OK?" I managed.

She will be, she is just sedated. She will wake in a few hours, the voice responded.

I let out a long sigh of relief. She was okay. I looked at her. Her soft features, her dark hair brushing her small nose. I held her in the cold.

Does she have the stones? The voice asked.

I felt around her pockets. I pulled out the mind stone but could find no others.

The voice spoke in my ear.

It could be worse. As long as he doesn't have this *stone, my plan can still be followed.*

What plan?

Get her to safety. Now, the voice commanded. I listened.

We flew further west, Nova lying bundled warmly in front of me. I held on to her and used my voice (and mind) to signal the dragon's directions.

When Nova awoke she nearly fell off the dragon. She jerked awake and squealed.

"Where am I?!" She turned and looked at me behind her and smiled. "Aww, you came!" she said, trying not to laugh.

My god she smelled so good. Like morning dew and fresh spring water. I rolled my eyes at her and she turned around to take in the view. We could see in the distance the sun halfway up in the sky, shining light on a field, just barely in view. Mountains stretched in miles all around us. I wanted to ask Nova what had happened but maybe I would put that on pause.

The voice echoed in my mind: *these are not your friends.*

I wanted Nova to be more than that. She stretched her arms upward as I told the dragon to dive. We soared as the morning mist dissolved revealing glittering creeks and stunning waterfalls in the mountains below. Her hair blowing, I relished in the moment. We flew in and out of the clouds, like we were on a ride. I wished it could last forever.

They are not your friends.

I ignored it. Though it was getting progressively harder.

Nova clutched the dragon's neck as we flew down again. I held her waist. It was perfect.

We flew for what felt like days. The sun dipped in front of us as we reached the edge of the border mountains.

A grassy field and a couple of oak trees lined the horizon. We landed there. A few hundred yards away from the treacherous mountain range. Were we the first ones to live past that distance? I had so many questions for Nova, and for myself.

Was the voice wrong? Nova really seemed like my friend. The others had pushed her away. We were always fighting. Was the voice right? Was Nova the only one who was my friend? I pushed those thoughts away and would ponder them later, just so I could have a less good night's sleep.

We made camp for the night. We drank some drought, ate some food, and I told her about what had happened since she left. But she would not elaborate. She told me bits and pieces. The man in the hood. How he took the other 4 gems. She wouldn't tell me who he was, but she seemed to know him. She spoke about his appearance and the magic sedation poison and pills, but she was reluctant to say further on who the man was. Whenever I asked her who he was, hurt seemed to seep from her eyes, but still she would say nothing. I put my arm around her as we sat under a large oak tree.

"You never did tell me who you like," she said slyly, wanting names.

As the sun sunk further down, making the sky gold and pink, my arm was around Nova. No matter how much she got on my nerves, I wanted to be with her. It was her I liked. Not Valen, nor Rune. Not Ashen either. It was Nova.

I looked over at her. Wind blowing her hair around her face. I looked into her eyes.

"Who is it, Rob?" she smirked.

It all seemed so perfect. I almost forgot we were following a dangerous prophecy, our group torn apart despite the words: *band together for ye need fight.*

I forgot the crazy wizard and the voice in my head.

All around me were wild flowers, a sunset in the distance, and a dragon grazing like a horse behind us. And Nova. There was Nova and me, under a big oak tree.

I leaned over and kissed her.

We sat there together for a while in silence, until I broke it.

"Never, call me *Rob* again."

She laughed. It sounded so pretty.

And off we drifted to sleep. Under the starry sky, just her and I.

Chapter 19
Your Hamster is Very Slow

The wizard was acting strange once again. He sipped his tea, or he thought he had. No one broke it to him that his cup was empty and that he was holding it upside-down.

He gently placed the cup down and clasped his hands together, as if he were deep in thought. No one wanted to know what was going on in that head of his, but Rune felt it would move things along much faster if she just asked.

"What exactly are you pondering?" she asked, irritated.

The wizard chuckled, bearing missing teeth. "My, my, curious, are we? Fear not, young girl. I've got an excellently excellent explanation to answer your question, if you'd allow the hamster to continue to run!" he said.

Rune gave him a strange look. "The hamster?" she questioned, still at least thankful the man was speaking understandable sentences.

The wizard pointed a gnarled finger to one of his many strange paintings. This was one of an obese hamster running on a wheel, encased in something pink and noodle-like that looked suspiciously like brain matter.

"Oh, yes! Why, everyone has a hamster. A small little rodent that runs on a wheel, powering one's train of thought. You've got a hamster! I bet it's bright pink! You seem like you would enjoy that colour. Allow me to think for a moment," the wizard said in a sing-song voice.

"I *hate* pink," Rune muttered.

Valen leaned next to Rune. "He's as mad as a hatter! We should go," he whispered.

The wizard frowned. "Why, you silly boy. I don't enjoy hats very much. They restrict my hamster. How could one not know such a thing? Your hamster must be quite slow," he said, staring at Valen.

Valen went red in the ears. Rune and Ashen snickered.

"Forget that! We need help!" Valen said, beyond embarrassed.

"Ah, yes. Not another word, boy. I've got the solution. My hamster has saved the day yet again!" The wizard exclaimed. At that very moment, the wizard's expression became serious. He laced his fingers once again and began to pace. "You've all gotten yourselves into a bit of a doozy, haven't you? Not to worry, my friends. Your traitor will reveal themselves quite soon."

"She already has. It's Nova. After the crap she pulled with the gems? Pretty obvious," Ashen said.

The wizard sighed, twirling his cup on the table. "I

don't believe it is who you think."

"But I don't understand. We can't agree on anything; maybe what the prophecy meant is that we'd all turn on each other. Maybe we're *all* traitors," Valen offered.

"Spoken like a true traitor," Rune muttered.

Valen stood and launched himself at Rune in a pathetic attempt to defend what little dignity he had left after the hamster fiasco. Rune yawned and raised a hand. At her command, vines shot from the ground and wound themselves tightly around Valen's writhing body. One coiled around his ankle, sending him to the ground. He spat a colorful stream of violent curse words towards Rune, who shut him up by coiling a vine around his mouth. To make it worse, the vines began to sprout pink aster flowers, making Valen look like a garden mound.

Rune and Ashen were busy cracking up when the wizard silenced them with a screech similar to that of a distressed owl.

"You're all wrong. Flower boy, there is only one traitor. And you?" he said, pointing to Rune. "Excellent work. You've made this silly boy look like quite the fool."

Valen cursed through his vine gag.

"Now, allow me to say something. It would be far better for you all to split up. Work towards the same goal, but split up. Fighting amongst yourselves does no good, I promise you. The traitor is one, not all. Please do remember this," the wizard said.

Ashen and Rune shared a look.

The wizard waved his hand and as if it was creating from nothing at all, a concentrated bright light only about the size of a coin appeared in front of them. The light grew until it was about as tall as Rune. It was bright, but not blinding.

"Please step through, children," the wizard said.

Rune waved a hand and the vines binding Valen's body disintegrated, leaving behind a single aster flower on the floor.

He vaulted up and shot Rune a withering glare before he took his place in front of the light. The three prepared to step through just as the wizard opened his mouth to say something for a final time.

"Do be careful, my young friends. Wield your powers, hold your weapons. You'll need them. The fall of the sectors is near. But be brave, children. That is something they cannot take away from you."

The three had already stepped through the portal of light before they could ask the wizard what exactly he had meant.

After Rune's eyes adjusted, she looked around. By her surroundings, she guessed she was in-

"Sector two," Ashen said, interrupting her thoughts. There was something about his tone. It was heavy, almost sad.

They were standing in sector two, home of the Aquas. Or at least what was left of it. It's trademark glass and steel buildings were destroyed, bits of them littering the ground wherever you looked. But that wasn't the worst of it.

The bodies.

Oh, how many there were. On the ground, dead without a doubt. Stab wounds. Gun shot wounds. Each and

every person on the ground was adorned in blue camouflage uniforms. Some still carried their weapons, some were curled up with closed eyes and peaceful expressions, as if they had simply fallen asleep and would wake up at any moment. Some's eyes were still open and so painfully lifeless, their faces still wearing the horrified expression they wore as they died.

"Oh no," Rune said, choken up. Valen immediately wiped his tears, but Ashen let them flow freely.

"What happened?!" he cried, falling to his knees.

Rune walked over to a fallen soldier and caressed her face. Rune shut the woman's eyes and swiped the star-shaped medal clipped to her uniform. "A medal of Valor," she said quietly, a tear rolling down her cheek.

Ashen was now sobbing.

Rune clipped the woman's medal of valor to her own shirt. She would keep it. She would keep it for the woman, as a reminder of her sacrifice and bravery. She now understood what the wizard had said as they stepped through the portal. *Be brave... that is something they cannot take away from you.*

"What's going on?" Valen asked quietly. Rune dried her tears.

"It appears the sectors have gone to war," said a gravelly voice behind them.

Chapter 20
The Prisoner is Back

Rune went still.

Judging by her surroundings, the bodies littering the ground and smoke billowing from what was once the vast metropolis of sector two, she didn't suspect another living being walked upon this ground.

Ashen dried his tears as he and Rune shared a worried look. At this very moment, someone stood directly behind them. This person could be anyone. They could be an enemy soldier, who contributed to this wreck.

Rune was the first to turn around, and she didn't exactly have a good feeling about what she saw. Only a few feet from her stood a man. He was caked in dirt, so it was difficult to make out his facial features. He seemed to have close-cropped grey hair and a scraggly goatee. The clothing he wore was stained and revolting, but seemed to be a faded shade of orange, bleached by the sun. Rune took a step back.

"Who are you?" Valen asked.

"Doesn't matter who I am." He pointed a liver-spotted finger at Rune. "Where is Robyn?"

Ashen stood at Rune's side. "Robyn is gone. What could you possibly want with them?"

The man stroked his beard and paced in small, slow circles. "Now, let's see. I am Robyn's *mentor*, and I need to discuss something... problematic. Such as the war," He said, gesturing to the wreckage behind the three.

"*Problematic?*! This isn't problematic, this is a grade A all-hands-on-deck disaster!" Rune shouted, surging forward.

She met the man's gaze, only about an inch from his face. His eyes were green, and cruel beyond belief. She could feel his breath on her face.

He simply laughed. Now that Rune was significantly closer to the man, she caught sight of a stained patch on his shirt, a symbol of some sort. An open eye, a crescent moon on each side. Rune backed up immediately.

"What's going on?" Ashen said.

"He's from Magi prison. Look at the emblem on his shirt," Rune answered, not looking away from the prisoner.

"Oh damn! That's a twist," Valen said. Rune kicked his ankle.

The prisoner stroked his chin. "Now, where did you say Robyn was? I need some good news."

❖❖❖

3 DAYS EARLIER

His footsteps reverberated across the corridor. He stared at his boots, as they revealed themselves from his cloak every time he took a step against the stone floor. At his sides stood two guards, alert and in uniform, guiding him to someone he had vowed to never see again.

Dave fiddled with his thumbs, eager yet nervous to meet the prisoner once again. When the guards came to halt before a massive stone door, he stopped in his tracks as well. One of the guards pulled a key from his pocket and it twisted the lock in the door with a click that echoed across the hall.

The doors were pushed open. At the pull of a lever, several sets of bars were raised, each clanking louder than the last. Finally, they arrived at the cell. Exactly where Dave needed to be.

It was a simple looking place. The cell which held the prisoner had nothing but a single window, which allowed the light of the moon to spill onto the floor, illuminating the prisoner's silhouette.

"You have fifteen minutes," one of the guards grumbled. They left Dave and the prisoner alone.

Dave felt an unsettling awareness of his own heartbeat.

"Hello, Dave," The prisoner said, not even bothering to turn to face his visitor.

"H-hello, your Excellency," Dave stammered.

The prisoner chuckled. "Oh, how refreshing it is to hear that after all these years. But alas, My reign is unfortunately over. Call me Zed."

"Al-alright Zed. I have a favor to ask," Dave said.

The prisoner sighed. "Why, of course you do. I don't get a single visitor for thirty years and the day I do, it's for a favor. Typical."

"I didn't mean to offend you, your excel- I mean, Zed. It's not a large favor."

"What is it, exactly?" the prisoner questioned.

"My niece, Nova, is on a quest. It's not the quest I'm worried about. It's the people she's questing with. This one, Robyn-"

Dave didn't get to finish.

"Ah, yes. My protege. I do hope they're doing well," Zed said wistfully.

Dave decided it would be wise not to question. Rather, he decided to get straight to the point.

"I want to make sure Nova is safe. I couldn't think of anyone better to help than you."

Zed was silent for a moment, as if pondering this.

The hall suddenly got extremely cold. Dave wrapped his cloak tighter around his body. "Why is it freezing?" he chattered. "Ah, forgive Ezra. She's in a mood," Zed said, yawning. Dave's mouth fell open. "Ezra, as in the *Snow Queen*?" he said, aghast. The snow queen, one of the most infamous criminals in all the sectors. A young girl born with extraordinary powers over the cold. She was known for freezing over three of the four sectors, killing thousands. She was dubbed the Snow Queen, and could be collected on villain cards, a popular children's collecting game of famous evil criminals on playing cards. Dave thought about Robyn's image plastered on one of those cards. The thought put him back on track.

"Now, Nova? How do I make sure she's safe?"

"Simple. Get me the stones. Five of them. You'll find them deep within the cavern of the golden dragon. Retrieve those, and Nova is good as safe," Zed answered.

Dave scratched his neck. "I-I don't know. That could be dangerous."

Zed snapped his fingers, and immediately Dave was put into a daze, victim of Zed's powerful mind control.

"You *will* get those stones, and you will leave me now. Do you understand?" Zed snapped.

Dave nodded, dazed.

He then left, his footsteps echoing back through the corridor, getting quieter as Dave got farther away. There was one thing that Dave didn't notice.

In all that had happened, he'd left Zed's cell door *wide* open.

chapter 21
Where is the Fifth Stone?

Uncle Dave walked back with the stones safely tucked into his pocket. *The prisoner is going to be so happy*, he thought. He had all of the stones that the prisoner asked for. He honestly felt bad for what he did to Nova, but technically he was doing it for her own good.

He walked through the empty woods with his hands in his pocket making sure the stones wouldn't fall out. He was on the way back to the prison to give Zed what he wanted. He wasn't quite sure what the prisoner would do with them, but that wasn't really his problem. As he was almost pulling into the prison, he saw Zed walking out. It seemed he had escaped.

"Zed! Wha..what how are you out? They let you out so soon?"

"I escaped, you left the cell door open, so I walked out. Then it took some effort to get by all the guards outside but mind controlling powers can handle that for you."

"Oh okay... okay. Anyways, I got the stones."

"Really? Show me."

Dave pulled the stones out of his pocket and handed them gently to Zed. Zed looked at the stones one by one. After counting only four, Zed's expression changed.

"THIS IS ONLY FOUR STONES, I SPECIFICALLY TOLD YOU THERE ARE FIVE!" Zed screamed.

Uncle Dave looked confused. "The girl only had four."

"No she did not, are you the one who has mind controlling powers? I made her keep the stones so I knew how many she had. And she had five."

"But you sure can still do a lot with the four."

"The fifth is the most powerful, the mind controlling one. With these four, I am limited. When I have the fifth, I can do many more powerful things!" Zed screamed.

"I'm sorry, I didn't know. She only handed me the four so I thought it was the four sector stones, I didn't realize there was also the rare mind controlling-" Zed cut Dave off.

"I DON'T CARE WHAT YOU THINK, I TOLD YOU THERE WERE FIVE"

"I'm sorry, I didn't know."

"Well, since you did not complete my request, I will not be making sure Nova is safe, instead I will do the opposite, I will make her suffer."

"No please, I still got you the four, please you can't, I still helped you!" Dave tried to grab the four stones from Zed.

"I said five so the deal is off. And don't you try to take these four from me, I still have a plan, a backup plan since what you did made my initial plan fail."

Zed walked off and left Dave to agonize behind him. Zed still had an idea of what to do with the four stones. He was going to establish a war between the sectors.

You may ask why? Well, these four sectors, the Aquas, Terras, Embers and Auras never accepted the rare power of mind control. Even Zed's own family thought of him as abnormal and never accepted him: because he wasn't one of them. The four sectors thought something was wrong with people who had mind control powers, so they made them go far away and didn't allow them to be around. Things were a little better now but Zed wanted revenge.

He was going to use the stones to put the sectors at war by using the stones in the opposite way that they were supposed to be used. His first plan was to mind-control the guards to let in an enemy army, then he would use the stones to make each of the sector's powers go down. Yes you could do that if you knew how, and since Zed was stuck in jail, there wasn't anything else to do but to research.

He would make it so that no one could use their powers to fight. And when you couldn't use your powers, you couldn't do much to fight back. This would cause agony and war between the sectors and that was exactly what Zed wanted.

Zed walked all the way back to the homes where all the sectors were peacefully living their normal lives. That was about to change soon.

He visited the guards of the sector walls and before they could say anything - he took control of their minds. *Open the gates*, he commanded.

And they did.

As the huge wrought-iron gates creaked open, Zed glimpsed his evil army, just beyond. They had arrived.

With a wave of Zed's hand, the army started marching forward. Small, mechanical steps. Mind-controlled steps. Tens, then hundreds, and more hundreds of Terras marched into the Aqua sector, wearing battle armor.

Zed snapped, and the side flanks of this army broke off and down the side streets. With an additional snap, rows of houses suddenly went up in flames.

Everyone came out of their homes and there was complete chaos. They tried to use their powers but they were unsuccessful.

Because Zed had been successful.

Zed ran into the throng. He ran through the bloody battle with glee, looking left and right at the destruction and soaking in the screams of terror echoing throughout the sector.

He didn't know how long he was running for. But at some point, it started to grow quieter. And quieter. The people who had been standing and screaming and fighting were now silent, on the ground, wrapped up in vines.

Eventually, he slowed down too. In the distance, he spotted three figures: people. They stared at the destruction around them. They looked horrified. Zed knew at once who they were. He walked up behind them. They seemed to be discussing something.

He cut them off - there was no point in letting them continue:

"It appears the sectors have gone to war."

On the Other Side

The group turned around.

They all stopped and stared at each other for a few seconds before saying anything.

"Who are you?" Valen asked.

"Doesn't matter who I am." He pointed a liver-spotted finger at Rune. "Where is Robyn?"

Ashen stood at Rune's side. "Robyn is gone. What could you possibly want with them?"

Zed stroked his beard and paced in small, slow circles. "Now, let's see. I am Robyn's *mentor*, and I need to discuss something... problematic with them. Such as this war," he said, gesturing to the wreckage behind the three.

"*Problematic?*! This isn't problematic, this is a grade A all-hands-on-deck disaster!" Rune shouted, surging forward.

She met Zed's gaze, only about an inch from his face. She flinched as she caught the small design on his shirt.

"What's going on?" Ashen asked.

"He's from Magi prison. Look at the emblem on his shirt," Rune answered, not looking away from the prisoner.

"Don't worry about the war. I know all about it," Zed said in a light tone.

Rune scoffed. "And how exactly do you know that?"

Zed responded quietly "Because I started it."

The group was dumbfounded.

Zed looked at the group again. "Now, where did you say Robyn was? I need some good news."

chapter 22
Walking Through Ruins

Nova and I walked through the Aqua sector. Piles of disintegrated rubble surrounded us. A small tear trickled down Nova's check as she looked around at the buildings she used to call home. To Nova, the piles of rubble still felt like home, in an odd sense.

I reached for Nova's clammy hand. I intertwined my fingers with hers. Nova and I walked in silence, not feeling any need for words to fill the silence in the air. Together, we walked past where the Aqua School, homes, and innocent people once stood.

Nova and I searched for survivors. I knew we would not find any. Yet, Nova found comfort in searching, even though we were faced with the impossible: finding survivors in the rubble and ruins after such a blow. I did not complain. We agreed to split up so we could search the vast ruins quicker. I searched the right side of the Aqua sector while Nova searched the left side.

As I walked alone, I thought about what could have caused this destruction of the Aqua sector. My thoughts were far too outlandish to be realistic. I thought of how the Terras could have gotten mad and leveled the Aqua sector. I even thought of how the Aqua leadership might have played a role in the destruction. I stopped thinking about causes. I realized my thoughts were pointless.

In the distance, I noticed a small patch of green grass within the Aqua sector's borders. I ran towards the grass. I allowed myself to hope for survivors even if just for a second. As I ran, I thought of being teleported back in time. Back to when I ran to my induction ceremony. Not even ten months ago, but I felt like a different person in a different lifetime.

I arrived at the patch of grass and immediately saw a young boy, no older than eight, sitting alone in the grass. I looked at the boy. He did not look up.

"Hi, what's your name?" I asked the boy. The boy looked up at me and scrambled backwards.

"No, no, no, it's okay." I held up my hands defensively. "My name's Robyn."

The boy still did not answer.

"I'm just trying to help. What is this patch of grass?" I persisted.

After several moments, the boy finally responded. "I don't know. I stood here when the attack happened. My parents, are they alive?"

I hesitated. "I'm not sure. You're the only survivor I've found. Who did this? Who attacked?"

"I don't know," the boy responded.

"That's okay. You need to get out of here. Trust me. If you are one of the last Aquas then you are in danger," I told the boy. The boy looked around, not knowing where to go.

"Just run!" I said.

As the boy ran away towards the Terra sector, I realized he never told me his name. I walked back to where Nova and I said we would meet. I found Nova waiting for me.

"Did you find anyone?" Nova asked.

"No," I lied.

Nova looked disappointed. We walked for a few more minutes in silence. We came to a fork in the road. Nova guided me to the right. After a few steps, Nova stopped. Nova looked ahead into the distance at a pile of rubble. I nudged Nova's arm.

"That is... That was my house," Nova whispered, just loud enough for me to hear.

I didn't say anything. Instead this time, I guided Nova to the rubble in which her house once stood. Once Nova and I stood in front of where Nova's house once loomed, we stopped. Again, we didn't say anything for several minutes. The silence seemed to be all that needed to be said.

"My family..." Nova started.

"They probably made it out in time," I finished, not caring if I lied as long as it gave Nova a little comfort.

Nova and I sat down in the dust covered sector.

"Who do you think did this?" Nova asked as she looked around at the destroyed sector.

"I don't know. But I do know that we will stop them. I promise," I replied.

"How? How can we stop whoever did this? Our group can't even get along," Nova asked.

Again, I could only offer Nova silence.

Eventually, side-by-side, Nova and I carefully walked through the crumbled doorway and into the remains of the house. I could barely make out where the modest kitchen, bathrooms, and bedrooms once stood. No one remained inside. Or so we thought.

Nova walked inside another crumbled room and screamed in horror. Nova's scream echoed through the air. I rushed over and found her running out of the room.

"He's . . . He's here," she said while gasping.

After a minute, out came Nova's Uncle Dave.

"YOU!" I yelled. "You fought Nova in the cave!" I continued.

"I'm sorry Nova. I truly am. I know I treated you poorly-" Uncle Dave started.

"Be quiet! Stop trying to act like the good guy when you're not!" Nova said.

"We don't have time for this. Again, I'm sorry, but we have more pressing matters," Uncle Dave replied.

"More pressing? More pressing than telling us why you were torturing me in that cave?" Nova scoffed.

"Yes. Unfortunately, we do." Uncle Dave replied.

"Well, let's hear it then," Robyn said.

With a deep breath, Uncle Dave said: "The sectors are at war."

chapter 23
Arrest or Kill?

Back where the four elements lived, a council meeting was held. It was exclusive to the four council members. Marina was an Aqua, Zephyr was an Aura, Vulcan was an Ember, and Gaia was a Terra. They all had a very big issue to discuss.

"Now that everyone is here, we can start the meeting," Councillor Marina said, very prominently.

Everyone took their usual seats at the table. Usually there were some other high powered people sitting there too but this was an emergency meeting, so only the four heads of powers could come.

"The issue on the table is," Councillor Zephyr read off a piece of paper. "Robyn, and their powers."

"A mind controlling witch is a menace. We cannot let them walk around freely," Councillor Vulcan brought up.

"I agree, that *thing* is too dangerous to have just walking around," Councillor Gaia added.

"We need to do something about Robyn, but what?" Vulcan questioned.

"I believe that we need to take serious action," Marina alluded.

"We need to send Robyn to prison. They are too dangerous to be free." Gaia was pondering many options in her head before coming up with this one.

"While I agree that Robyn is dangerous, I do think that they deserve worse than just prison. A death sentence is the only way to contain this type of power," Zephyr sneered.

"Have you no decency Zephyr? They are just a child. Killing is a crime," Vulcan tried to defend Robyn's life.

"Robyn is sixteen, not a child. And remember what happens to people with these powers? Many years ago there were five sectors," Marina started. "As we know there were the four natural elements, but there was another tribe. The mind and soul tribe. They lived in unison until one day the people with the mind and soul powers started an uprising. They destroyed everything, and so they had to be killed off. Fifty years ago, another one came into existence. He also went on a quest, and ultimately turned evil. Instead of killing him, we put him in prison. Now, Robyn comes along. We don't know what they're capable of. Have we learned from our mistakes? We have to kill them. It's the only way to keep everyone safe."

"Killing Robyn will only lead to more arguing and death in the future. It won't fix anything," Gaia responded.

"I agree. Now, we are more trained and advanced than back then. We have ways to make sure they don't step out of line... It is decided... Robyn will be sent to prison and monitored carefully," Vulcan concluded.

"What? No, we never decided that. Robyn cannot be allowed to continue living. It must be a death sentence. Nothing less," Marina and Zephyr argued.

A fight broke out between the council members. Gaia and Vulcan both agreed that Robyn deserved a prison sentence while Marina and Zephyr thought they deserved death.

Word soon got around that the council members were arguing viciously. Although no one knew how because they were in a locked room with no windows and no possible way of someone hearing them. Some people of the sectors decided to take action. They used this fight to finally take personal revenge against other elemental sectors by whom they felt wronged.

"Oh, those Aquas are going down!" a man yelled.

He looked as if he was already in his own personal war. His shirt was dirty and torn up and his pants were a faded blue color. His hair was extremely untidy, like he hadn't brushed it in at least ten years.

He ran into his house, or shack, and grabbed a bottle of wine. He had many. The man ran to the Aqua/Ember border and held out his hand. He lit the bottle on fire and threw it over the wall.

It landed on top of an Aqua house. The whole thing exploded. The man looked extremely upset when he found out the house was deserted.

"You've gotta be kiddin' me! I wanted to see some Aquas get what they deserved!" The man was extremely unstable from losing everyone and everything he had ever loved.

So much fighting was happening that some people lost their sense of mortality, they did whatever was necessary to make their point. Many people died and more people continued to die.

There was no end to this war in sight. No one was safe during this time and it looked like no one would be safe for a while.

※※※

Nova's uncle Dave was explaining how the war that was going on started. I almost liked the idea of war, even though I knew I shouldn't.

It is right to like it. If it pleases you, so be it. The voice knew what I was thinking.

"So anyway," Dave continued. "Some people now are doing what your parents did to those Em-" He was cut off by Nova's stare and head tilt towards me.

"What about Embers?" I asked, very skeptical of what they knew that I didn't.

"Oh, nothing. I'll tell you more later," Nova looked more normal now. Normal as in she didn't look like she was keeping a secret. Kind of.

"Promise?"

"Promise."

"What, I can't hear you over all the loud banging noises!" I yelled, not able to hear Nova say whether or not she promised to tell me more about what her uncle Dave was talking about.

On the Other Side

"I said I promise to tell you more later." Nova screamed back.

There was no silence anywhere. Booms, thuds, slams were all that could be heard. Me, Nova, and Uncle Dave sat at Nova's dining room table. Her parents could not be found. I understood Nova's worriedness for them being missing or possibly dead because I had to go through that with my own parents. I've been living on my own since I found out they were dead.

Even being an only child with no siblings, I never felt like the favorite child. Even though I may not have had the best experiences with my mom and dad, of course I still missed them.

But now I have no time to look into the past. I must stay focused on the present and think about the future. *My* future.

Chapter 24
I Go On a Killing Spree

Nova and I got onto my dragon's back again. There was something unsettling about the day, but I didn't fully know what yet. Was it the loud noises? Maybe.

The dragon rose into the air once more, and we were off to the sky.

We stayed close enough to see what was happening in the sectors, but high enough that they wouldn't see us very quickly.

"Robyn," Nova started. "What will happen to us? I mean Embers and Aquas hate each other." Her head rested on my shoulder, and she was holding on to my waist.

"Well, I'm not really an Ember, am I?" I gave myself a small smirk that left quickly after. "I'm a mind freak. And that's even worse." I felt her move behind me.

"Robyn, you're not a freak. You're just different. And that's okay," she assured me.

"Really? You like being with a freak?" I ask her.

"I love it," she told me. "And I really like you." Her words made me smile.

"What kind of like?" I joked around with her a bit. She laughed at this.

"I *like*-like you, Robyn."

"I really like-like you, too." I felt her hug me from behind upon hearing the words leave my mouth. I sighed, comforted by the fact that at least I had someone.

The conversation was a bit slower after that, and we were now hovering over sector three, where, to my displeasure, the Terras and the Auras were in the midst of a battle.

"We have to go help Rune," Nova told me. I nodded my head, and we looked for the dark skinned brunette via the air.

We found her fighting with an Aura in a park. I commanded the dragon to let us down by her, and it followed its orders. I hopped off the dragon and turned to help Nova off.

Once we were both off the dragon and safe on the ground, we looked at each other.

"Do I get a kiss for good luck?" I asked Nova. She gave me a cheeky grin, but pressed her soft lips to mine. We stayed like that for a bit until Nova pulled away.

"Now let's go, we have to help Rune," she said and we rushed to her side.

Rune was trying to capture an Aura in vines when we got there. But the Aura kept struggling.

Stop struggling and stay in the vines, was the command I gave. And Rune looked confused when they followed it. She turned around and saw us. She sighed in relief.

"Thanks Robyn, for a second I didn't know if I could get them to stop moving," she said. She looked at Nova and nodded her head. Clearly, having nothing to say to her.

"Watch out Robyn," Rune suddenly said, pointing behind me. I turned and ducked just in time to avoid being punched by the guy that was about to attack me. I quickly stood back up and returned a punch, knocking him unconscious.

That felt like a wake up call.

As if the world was telling me; Robyn you're in the middle of a war, you don't have time for conversing with your friend and girlfriend.

Girlfriend?

She isnt your girlfriend. And the other is not your friend.

Ugh, stupid voice. I shook my head, ignoring it.

"We should really start helping," I said. Nova and Rune nodded their heads in agreement. Rune ran off into battle and I was left face to face with Nova.

"Here, this is yours," she handed me a purple stone. The mind stone. I looked at her and took it.

"Thanks Nov," I smiled slightly at her. I hugged her tightly. "I'll meet you here after this is done, okay?" I told her. She nodded her head and slowly went into battle also.

I turned this time to the crystal dragon.

Go kill some Auras, okay?

I ordered it. It nodded its head and flew off. I saw it burn an Aura on the way. Then it was my turn to go and fight. Sorry Valen.

A couple of Auras, a boy and a girl, in their twenties

(maybe?) made a gust of wind push me over.

I tried to get off the ground, but I was being firmly held down. I prayed that Nova was okay, and focused my attention back to the Auras in front of me. Suddenly, I felt furious. Their attempt to restrain me was pathetic and deserved to be punished.

Robyn, you know what to do. You know how to get free. Do it. You know what I'm telling you to do.

The voice sounded more persuasive at the moment, and it took me over. As if it was controlling me, and guiding my fury. I got into the boy's head.

He seemed to be in a daze. He had stopped using his powers. The girl beside him ignored him and kept me on the ground.

The boy returned with a pretty sharp stick. I smiled evilly.

You know what to do.

I looked at the girl.

She thought he would kill me?

She was wrong.

Her small smirk of victory was quickly replaced by a small gasp. Her face paled and she fell limply to the ground.

The boy's stick was through her heart. And her blood started to stain her gray top.

I got up from the ground and dusted myself off.

The boy, who had now regained full control of his mind, fell to his knees.

"Did you love her?" I asked him. I spoke as I started to circle them.

"Yes," the boy breathed.

"Then why don't you join her? In the land of forever. You could be together for eternity. I'm sure she would really adore seeing you again." I paused. Reaching out a single finger, I lifted his chin so he could look at me. I turned my head slightly to the side. "Or maybe she wouldn't. I mean, you did murder her." I flicked my finger off of his chin.

His eyes were filled with tragedy. "It's all up to you," I concluded.

The boy thought for a second. He took the red ended stick out of the dead body, wincing as he did. He took a deep breath and closed his eyes. I looked away, and when I looked back, he laid beside her.

I took a deep breath.

Well done Robyn. Your persuasion skills are getting better.

Thanks, I replied to the voice. I grinned, feeling a little smug.

I rushed back into battle quickly after, killing a few Auras. Suddenly, I had a really bad gut feeling. Was it because I had just brutally killed a couple?

A senior?

Some younger kids also?

No, it wasn't because of that. I had no need to kill anyone, but it was a war. What did you want me to do? Eat cupcakes?

I ran down the unfamiliar streets. I needed Crystal, my dragon. Yes, I had finally thought of a name for him. And I personally thought that the name suited him. You know, because he was a crystal dragon!

Gosh, I did get so distracted.

Robyn you can call Crystal. Use the gem.

Calling a magical dragon by using a magical gem. Seemed legit. So I did. I channeled all my energy.

CRYSTAL, COME HERE!

A bolt of purple lightning struck beside me. And after a minute, his long crystal wings that shone like the sun, appeared by my side. I quickly got on his back and gave him instructions to bring me to Nova.

Silently observing the battle from the sky, there were quite a few dead bodies, from both sectors it looked like.

And then I saw her. Crystal brought me down, but I rushed off before we had even touched the ground.

Nova seemed to be fighting someone. That someone had brown hair and… no.

Rune.

For some reason, they both seemed furious. They were battling with everything they had. But why? They looked like they were capable of killing each other. How had this happened so quickly? And then Rune struck out at Nova with a vine that twisted all the way up her body and around her neck.

"No!" I screamed. "Nova!"

I started sprinting, not believing my eyes.

I pushed past people, trying to get there. Around the heads in the crowd, I watched the branch tighten its grip. I watched Rune narrow her eyes in concentration.

I tried to run faster.

But I was too late. Rune was driven. Then, she did it.

Nova fell to the ground, her ink black hair spilling out around her. The earth seemed to open up, like an enormous shark's maw, and swallow her whole. She sunk Nova into the ground.

Still a distance away, I stopped running in my tracks, unleashing a guttural scream.

Rune's concentration broke, distracted by the noise, and she fixed me in her gaze.

Her cruel expression faded, slowly turning to fear as she saw my reaction. Nova disappeared completely into the ground. And Nova turned to look back at me, expectant.

I was too late.

All I had done was watch.

chapter 25
I Lose It

You know that prolonged beeping sound, the one that would come on during a show if a character said a bunch of obscenities in a row? Yeah, queue that.

I sprinted over to Rune, screaming.

"What did you do?!" I yelled as I approached her.

"I'm sorry Robyn, I had to," Rune said, but only apologizing for my sake, not Nova's.

"What did you do?!" I repeated louder. "Where is she?!" I spoke on the verge of tears. A bubble of anger formed deep in my stomach.

"She's gone. I- I-" she stammered.

"I-I…" I mocked her, pouting. "WHAT DID YOU DO!" I screamed.

"It's not what it looks like!"

"Well what *does* it look like to you?" my voice quivered. "To me, it looks like you killed her!" Tears welled in my eyes. "Bring. Her. Back." I was trembling out of anger and fear, worried she might truly be gone.

"I can't Robyn, I'm sorry!" She was really trying to sell it.

Not your friends. I knew then that the voice was right. Your friends don't kill your other friends.

"Why…" I wanted to say more but trailed off, it was too painful.

"I had to!"

"Give me one reason why."

"Because, I…" she faltered.

"How could you?! She was the only thing left in my life that I cared about," I spoke so harshly that Rune winced. "If you even had one shred of decency, you would've run for the hills as soon as the deed was done!"

"Robyn," her voice turned impatient. "You don't understand, you're blinded by your feelings."

"I am not, you are the one who is blinded, by your lack thereof!" I could feel my blood begin to boil, I was crying and yelling. Anger and sadness, I could not differentiate any longer. It all blended together, forming a big ball of pain. "You," I said between sobs. "Monster!"

"She was the traitor!"

"That is not true!" I fell to my knees at the resting place of Nova. There was no body, just a rough dirt patch. I dug ferociously. Clinging to whatever hope I had left. I cried as I quickly realized there was no hope.

I turned to face Rune once again.

"You have three seconds," I spoke.

"For what?!" Rune asked, scared.

"One,"

"For what!?" She repeated, though I was not talking to her. I couldn't.

"Two,"

"Robyn, please don't hurt me!"

"Three."

I used that pit of emptiness inside and filled it with magic. I pulled out the Mind gem and held it outstretched. I forced all the Aura troops to flee sector 3.

I was so upset that my power multiplied. Never had I controlled more than one person at once. Now, I was forcing hundreds to do my bidding. For a moment I felt better.

I turned my head a fraction of a degree and stared into Rune's eyes. So much hatred filled me. I suddenly blamed everything on her, not depending on facts.

Get revenge. I will help you. Prove to Nova you care. Care deeply.

I do, I responded to the voice.

Then hurt the traitor. And then become one in everyone's eyes, for thou shall win and prove them wrong.

I didn't quite understand everything they had just said. Though one thing I did, I would hurt Rune. Death was too easy, not quite painful enough. I needed her to suffer, suffer like I did.

I wormed my way into Rune's mind. My gaze was unwavering.

She did feel guilty. She thought she did the right thing, oh, I would prove her wrong.

That guilt she felt. Triple it.

Rune began to cry.

"What are you doing to me?" she said in a strained voice.

"Hurting you."

"You don't want to do this," she sobbed.

"Oh, I think I do." I didn't think so. I knew so.

I forced her to her knees.

You will pay in great. The people you love will pay as well. You are my hostage. And they are the ransom.

She cried aloud. Begging me not to hurt them, to take her life instead.

"It's your fault." I whispered.

"Please!" She continued to beg.

I willed her hands to close around her throat. She stopped speaking.

"You took the life of the only person that could save you. With her infinite compassion, she would forgive you. I will not. I will break you like you broke me," I threatened.

I spoke inside her head again. *Why did you have to do it? Don't force them to pay for your mistakes. You killed the only person left who loved me. I will do the same to you.*

"By the end of it all," I spoke aloud once more. "You will feel the same as me. Alone. No one alive will love you."

You see, you fulfilled the prophecies line. The traitor is the killer, not the stealer. Without those gems we were able to free the Crystal Dragon. Don't you see? You killed Nova for her good deed. That makes you the villain. You kill the innocent.

Rune bawled her eyes out as she apologized over and over.

"Not gonna cut it. We're way past sorry."

I tightened her grip on her own throat.

"Agh!" she gagged as I caused her airforce trauma.

I released her grasp. I urged her to feel pain all over. She keeled over sideways, thrashing and writhing in pain. I stopped it. I willed her to feel remorse so great it would eat her from the inside out.

She cried inconsolably, the same as I did on the inside.

I wanted her to hurt like I did. I had thought, just for a second, that the voice was wrong. But no, it was right, these were not my friends. It hadn't done me wrong. That's when I decided I would trust it completely.

I held the stone as I commanded her to bury herself waist deep in the ground.

"How does it feel?" I asked, struggling to force the word out. I was using so much energy. My muscles were tight everywhere.

She strained and tried to claw her way out. She tried to get free of my control. To stop herself from being buried alive, but she couldn't. I was so filled with every emotion that ranged from anger to enjoyment. I wanted to see her suffer.

I stopped her crying, so she could watch with a crystal clear view. She looked at me, tears trying to escape. An invisible dam stopped them. I turned her line of sight to the battlefield.

The Auras had returned.

I forced her to watch. I made her pay.

"It's all your fault," I said, soothing any doubts that she wasn't in the wrong. She not only would watch them die, and do nothing, as I did with Nova. But she would help me, with no way to stop it. For I had the mind gem. I could get her to do anything and everything I wanted her to do within her power.

Without resisting.

"You don't have to do this!" Rune yelled.

"Neither did you."

She sobbed with dry eyes. I admit it looked weird, but she needed to see this. To do this.

I turned and walked toward the battlefield. I stopped just before I was out of earshot. I summoned my dragon and got atop him. I turned him so that I was facing Rune. Still emerged in the ground. I got her to bury herself. Up to her neck in the ground, with her hands free a few inches in front of her.

A tear escaped my eye and I smiled. I would avenge Nova.

I spoke to Rune, the last words she would hear before she was broken.

"Let's have some fun."

Chapter 26
I Blow Up a City

"I thought you said sector three was in danger," Councillor Marina said, clearly annoyed. No one had time for this.

"That isn't the problem," Councillor Gaia said quietly, staring at her sodden boots.

"Then what is?!" Councillor Vulcan cried.

Councillor Gaia crossed her arms over her stomach and looked up at her fellow council members.

"Sector three is gone. The witch wiped it off the map."

The sound of Councillor Zephyr stuttering broke the shocked silence.

"B-But how?" Councillor Vulcan asked as the rest of the group tried to pick their jaws off the ground, still stunned.

The council had reluctantly reconvened because Councillor Gaia had insisted that the entire kingdom was in danger. What everyone had not realized was that they were in the midst of a much, much larger threat than each other.

Councillor Gaia wiped tears from her eyes before responding. "The witch controlled our own people to level the entire sector. They were riding on The Dragon of Crystals and defeated another sector's dragon. They are powerful beyond our imaginations. The prophecy is coming true. They even wield the sword of Ragnarok."

Gaia took a seat, still shaken by the words that had just come out of her mouth. All the other council members did the same as they contemplated what to do next.

"We need to stop this witch before it gets out of hand," Councillor Marina said.

Councillor Vulcan nodded. "Who knows who or what the witch will target next? They are on a rampage now. We have to stop them before it gets too late."

The four council members all nodded their heads.

"We might not have a place left to save soon. We need to take action. Violent or not. It doesn't matter now," Councillor Zephyr put in.

The meeting adjourned and they all silently agreed to attempt to call a truce between all of the sectors. For the good of the kingdom, they hoped, prayed that the full force of the kingdom would be enough to stop the controller of the Mind Gem and the Rider of The Dragon of Crystals at their full power.

They all prayed silently.

1 HOUR EARLIER

"Let's have some fun."

I flicked my hands and the nearest Terras began to

completely destroy the entire sector. They used earthquakes and sinkholes after demolishing buildings and the ground was ripped apart. I smiled cruelly through tears.

I climbed onto my crystal dragon and my eyes narrowed with anger and determination. I knew what I would have to do. I told the dragon to shoot into the sky and he breathed fire, roasting the Terras still in their houses and cooking the ground with lava-hot fire.

I laughed as I snapped my fingers and another group of Terras lifted up the ground they were standing on and raised it up. They let it go when it was over a hundred feet in the sky, and it exploded when it hit the ground, rocks and debris flying everywhere, most of the city leveled. I told the dragon to ram through the main building of the Terras and he shot like a bullet towards it, roaring so loud the world shook.

He slammed directly into it, completely destroying the most important building in the city. The glass and brick flew everywhere as we continued our rampage. My dragon crashed through building after building, scorching people and then eating them. The Terras that I wasn't controlling yet tried to fight back and raised boulders and shot them at me.

I looked back at Rune, and smiled. She was shaking with tears streaming down her face. I relished in her pain. I made her feel like how I felt when she killed the only person who I loved. Who loved me.

I dodged a huge boulder with ease and yelled as my dragon roared. He crashed directly onto one of the Terras and spit fire everywhere. I jumped off and drew my sword.

The first Terra ran towards me, his sword raised. I side-stepped his clumsy swing and stabbed him in the chest. He fell to the ground and I kicked him away.

I cut the head off of the second Terra, and controlled the last to jump into the fire that my dragon just happened to breathe. I felt no mercy and regret. They take something away from me, I take everything from them. And then destroy them.

I rose out of the massacre, yelling as my dragon roared and blew torrents of red-hot flames at buildings and people alike.

I slammed the mind gem into the pommel of my sword for some reason and the entire sword glowed.

When the glow dimmed, I was holding a huge black bladed sword with red webbed through the hard material, with the purple mind gem glowing brighter than ever in the middle of the pommel of my sword. Oh, also, the sword was glowing with blue flames.

I heard battle cries and battle horns in the distance. The army had arrived. Finally.

I roared alongside my dragon and we dived towards the rows of shields, spears and swords. My dragon smashed directly into the middle of the pathetic shield wall of the army, and I jumped into battle with a cry of laughter.

The huge sword felt like an extension of my arm as I sliced and slashed through the countless soldiers. A spear shot towards my head and I caught it mid-air. I threw the offending spear back, and it hit the soldier right between the eyes and went through his helmet and gave him a free head piercing.

On the Other Side

A really dumb warrior shot a huge boulder at my crystal dragon. It opened its mouth and swallowed it whole with no problem. My dragon trampled, ate, and cooked multiple battle weapons and countless enemy soldiers. The metallic smell of blood filled the air as my sword became an arc of destruction. I slashed, weaved and stabbed through the "powerful" army.

We had destroyed more than half the army when they called a retreat. I frowned and quickly got onto my dragon. We flew after them, and just as we were about to land in front of the army and kill the rest of them, a flying green and gold blur slammed into my dragon, nearly knocking me off. I snarled as I saw the Terra dragon climb up into the sky above my crystal dragon.

I looked back and saw a long cut on my dragon's side. I clenched my fists until my knuckles popped and I screamed in rage. I shot towards the smaller green and gold dragon with a Terra rider on its back. My dragon and the Terra dragon crashed together, two incandescent meteors colliding head-on. The dragons grappled, kicking each other with their hind legs.

Their talons screeched against the crystal dragon and the dragons broke apart. The green dragon was smaller than my dragon, but it was thicker in the shoulders and legs. I barely kept hold of Ragnarok as the two dragons clashed again, battering each other with terrible blows from both their feet and tails. My dragon swiped and then followed up with a huge torrent of fire, which singed the dragon rider. He nearly dropped his sword.

I roared as I jumped from the back of my dragon onto

the other dragon's back. I nearly lost my balance then thought about Nova, and how Rune cast her into the ground. I screamed with rage as power shook through me and I steadied myself. The dragon was flying around in circles now, trying to get me off, but I grabbed its horns to steady myself. I stabbed at the shocked dragon rider and he blocked my sword.

He got up and slashed at me, nearly taking my head off. I feinted a slash to the left, and then twisted my blade and slashed for the head. He smiled after he flicked his wrist and completely deflected my strike, almost as if he had predicted what I was going to do next. I realized I was outmatched. This man had too much training and experience.

But I didn't let that scare me.

He was advancing slowly, knowing he could beat me now. He was wrong. I smiled and jumped off his dragon. His eyebrows raised as I plummeted towards the ground, looking like I was about to die. At the last moment, my crystal dragon swooped in and caught me.

We shot back up to the green and gold dragon up above, and as we passed them, I lashed out with Ragnarok. The blade's razor-sharp tip cut through the armor of the dragon relatively easily, and as my blade found flesh, the dragon roared in agony. I rose up on my crystal dragon and slashed fiercely at the rider. He slapped the flat of my sword with his own and furrowed his brow in confusion.

I smiled wickedly as I took control of his dragon and they began to plummet towards the ground. I let the dragon live, albeit wounded, but I killed the dragon rider. I controlled him to kill himself, impaling himself on his own sword. I didn't care at that point. All I cared about was revenge for Nova. I told my dragon to get me down to the ground.

I got back down to the ground in the midst of the ruined sector three, with the dead bodies of Terras and wrecked buildings all around me. I put down my huge sword. Nova was gone.

I felt the emotions pouring over me again like lava, burning me and hurting me. Nova was gone, I repeated in my head. I sat down on the ground beside my crystal dragon and began to sob...

chapter 27
I Relive the Worst Moment of my Life

I stood silently in the ruins of sector three. There were pieces of rubble everywhere, along with other things, like broken picture frames, and shattered glass. I looked at the mess around me.

To think that I'd done all of this.

I wanted to feel happy, because of how powerful I'd become, but all I felt was sadness. An emotion that I hadn't really felt for a while. Nova, the one person who loved me, who I loved back, was gone. The sadness I felt quickly turned into anger. Why did everyone I love have to die? It wasn't fair.

I heard footsteps behind me. I turned around to see the Prisoner slowly walking towards me.

"Robyn," he stated. "It doesn't have to be this way."

I stared at him blankly.

"You can fix all of this," he continued. "And then everything can go back to normal."

Normal? I didn't want everything to go back to *normal*. I hated normal. When things were normal, I was just an orphan who lived a sad and lonely life. I never wanted to have to go back to the way I'd lived for the past nine years.

I felt anger start to build up inside me. I was about to say something when I saw Ashen and Valen approach. I was pretty sure the only thing that could make me feel angrier than I was then, was Ashen.

"Robyn!" he shouted. "Look, I know you're upset, but what's the meaning of all this?" He gestured at the wreckage around us.

"Upset? You think I'm simply *upset*? I'm feeling resentful, agitated, exasperated, and extremely irate!" I yelled. I made Ashen punch himself in the face, and watched as his nose began to bleed.

"Robyn, enough is enough," barked Valen. "I know you're hurt, but you're going mad with power."

The Prisoner and the two boys looked at me with concerned expressions.

They're not your friends. They don't care about you.

The voice was right.

Put an end to them all. Robyn, if you kill all three of them, then I can tell you a way that you can get Nova and your parents back.

You can do that? I responded to the voice.

If you destroy these three then yes, I'm sure I can.

Those words are all it took to persuade me to defeat the Prisoner along with Ashen and Valen.

I couldn't contain my anger any longer. I used my powers to make Ashen toss his weapon on the ground in front of me. I picked up his shiny silver dagger. *Where did he get this from?* I thought.

It didn't matter. I focused my attention on the Prisoner. I knew he'd be the hardest to defeat, as he too had mind-control powers. Though it was hard to control someone's mind if they too were controlling yours. All I had to do was focus on controlling the Prisoner, while I took down Ashen and Valen at the same time. It would require a lot of concentration, but I had to do it; for Nova, for my parents, for myself.

I looked the Prisoner in the eyes, and he looked back at me. The look in his eyes didn't suggest he felt scared; it looked more like pity. The Prisoner's words rang in my ears: *It's dangerous to have so much power, so dangerous that you could possibly end up like me.*

What he said didn't matter anymore, I wanted to get my loved ones back.

I looked at Ashen and Valen. Ashen created a ball of fire in his hands, and Valen looked like he was about to send a tornado my way. I held up my dagger and got ready to use my powers.

Restrain the Prisoner, and then finish him off when the other two are gone, the voice told me.

I looked at the Prisoner and forced him to sit on the ground with his arms behind his back. I focused hard on my mind-control, when I glanced up at Ashen I saw that he was magnifying the big ball of fire in his hands. Being hit by that could kill me.

I could use my mind control to stop Ashen from throwing it, but if I stopped controlling the Prisoner for even a split second, he would have enough time to start controlling me. Ashen threw his fireball straight at me.

I quickly moved to the right, barely dodging it. The fire left burns on my stomach. Though I had to deal with the pain and concentrate on containing the Prisoner until I'd killed the other two.

Valen then sent a gust of wind in my direction, it blew me backward and I fell to the ground. I grabbed the Mind Gem from my pocket and clutched it in my fist. It made controlling the Prisoner a little bit easier. I needed a way to prevent Valen and Ashen from using their powers. I tried keeping the Prisoner's arms behind his back so that he couldn't take out the Fire and Air crystals he had in his pocket, but that didn't stop Ashen and Valen from rushing over and taking the gems themselves.

This battle wasn't completely fair. Two people of two different elements who each have their crystal, and a powerful mind-controller versus me. I didn't know what to do next. With my mind-control being solely focused on restraining the Prisoner, all I had was a dagger. At that moment, I decided close-range weapons weren't really my thing.

Crystal in one hand and my dagger in the other, I charged at the two boys. I dodged Ashen's fireballs and tried not to let Valen knock me over with his wind. I dodged attacks until I got close enough to the boys. I swung my dagger at Ashen, leaving a massive cut on his chest. I attempted to stab his shoulder, but he moved out the way and I got his arm instead. He screamed out in pain and fell to the ground. I'm pretty sure he was just unconscious, but it didn't matter, I would finish him off later.

I turned my attention to Valen, he was looking at me with a horrified expression on his face.

"Robyn, I- I don't understand why you would do this," he stammered. "Don't you think that you've gone too far?"

I shook my head. "I have to do this Valen."

I took my dagger to his leg, making a deep cut in his thigh. I hoped the pain would distract him from avoiding my next attack, and it did.

I swung the dagger as if it were a sword, and let it cut through Valen's wrist. He fell to the ground. I had completely detached his hand from his arm. That's enough, I thought, I didn't need to completely kill Valen, he would surely die of blood loss soon.

I looked back at the Prisoner. Thankfully, I had kept my concentration, and he was still on the floor trying to resist my powers.

Suddenly, I felt myself get weaker. *It must be all the power I'm using*, I thought. I held on tighter to my crystal. It didn't help that much.

Slowly but surely, The Prisoner began to resist my powers, and use his own. Before I knew it, he was standing on both feet. I was going to need every last bit of strength I had for this.

The Prisoner and I looked at each other intensely; we were both trying to control each other at the same time. I was using so much power that it was starting to hurt now. I felt pain coursing through my veins, but I kept my guard up. This was all for Nova.

I focused so hard that it felt like my brain would explode. The Prisoner was wincing, so clearly it was hurting him too. I held my crystal tighter, hoping it would give me more strength, but the pain was becoming unbearable. At the same time as I was concentrating, I looked at the Prisoner, who also looked like he was about to pass out. But just before he did, he forced out as much power as possible, and then, everything went black.

✤✤✤

Mother smiled down at me. "Are you ready to go hiking Robyn?"

I nodded and clapped my hands in excitement.

"Come and put your shoes on!" Dad shouted from the other room.

I rushed over to him and he helped me put on the sneakers. A few seconds later, my mother came over to us both.

"Are you ready to go?" she asked.

I put on my pink jacket and gave her a thumbs up. Dad squatted down so he was at eye level with me.

"Robyn. Just remember. *This section of the park is open to each of the sectors, so if you see someone who isn't an Ember, then stay close to me and mom and we'll walk in a different direction. OK?"*

I nodded, and we all walked out the door.

After a short walk to get there, we arrived at the hiking trail. My parents and I began our walk. I pointed out all the things I saw: flowers, birds, frogs, puddles. The most notable thing on the hiking trail was the river. It was a deep river with murky water and small fish that lived inside. I stopped walk-

ing so I could take a closer look at the water. It was too murky to see any fish.

"Don't get too close Robyn!" yelled my father. "The water is deep, so you must be careful!" He came over to me and picked me up. "Let's keep walking," he said.

We were all getting a little out of breath so we stopped for a rest. We sat under a large oak tree, located near the river. I found the water so fascinating, I couldn't quite understand why we were supposed to be so afraid of it.

"Mommy, why are we scared of water?" I asked.

"Well honey," my mother replied, "We're not afraid of water, we're just afraid of the Aquas. They have the ability to weaken our powers, as water and fire do not get along."

I nodded slowly, not fully understanding what my mom was telling me.

"Despite the Aquas being able to weaken our powers, us Embers are better than them."

"That's true," my father agreed.

"What was that about the Aquas?" a voice said. It came from the other side of the river.

My dad stood up and walked closer to the river, as did my mother.

"Just wait there, okay sweetie?" I smiled and did as I was told. My parents were still close enough for me to hear their conversation.

"Who's there?" my dad asked.

"Just the people who, according to you, aren't as good as the Embers," the voice replied.

A woman stepped into view from the other side of the river. She had long black hair and tan skin. A man, whom I assumed was the woman's husband, stepped out from behind a tree. He had grey hair and funny-looking glasses.

"You Embers are so full of yourself, aren't you?" he said.

"No sir, we didn't mean it in that way," father assured him. "We were just trying to explain to our daughter that-"

He was cut off by the woman. "All you're explaining to your daughter is how cocky and smug you Embers can be."

My father crossed his arms. "Based on this conversation alone, it doesn't seem like the Aquas are any better." His words were muffled but he'd said them loud enough for the couple to hear.

"Excuse me?" The woman knit her eyebrows. "I'll show you what an Aqua is capable of," she pointed her finger at the water in the river, and suddenly, two big waves pulled both my parents into it.

I hid behind a tree, hoping they wouldn't do the same to me. I knew neither of my parents were strong swimmers. I needed to save them, I just didn't know how. I peeked around the tree trunk to see what was happening.

My mom and dad kept trying to attack the Aquas with fire, but the water was weakening them. Every time they tried to swim to the riverbank, the Aquas kept washing them away with waves of water. Mother was gasping for air, but I'm pretty sure she was trying to tell me something. In between breaths she said:

"Robyn... run."

At this point, the Aquas were pretty much holding my parent's heads underwater. I couldn't just leave them, but there wasn't enough time to go and get help. I started to cry. I was literally watching my parents die. Never in my life had I felt so helpless.

I turned away, I couldn't watch this happen. I cried not only because I knew my parents were going to die, but also because I knew there was nothing I could do to save them. I was too much of a coward to confront the Aquas, but I couldn't really blame myself, I was only seven years old.

I heard the woman and the man laughing. "Come on, let's go." The man's voice said.

I ran out from behind the tree and peered into the murky water. "MOM! DAD!" I yelled. I splashed my hands in the water trying to grab ahold of them. "HELP!" I screamed. I sobbed, "Mom, dad, no."

No one had heard my call for help. I stayed by the river for the rest of the day, crying my eyes out while I reached into the water, hoping that my parents were still alive.

✢✢✢

"Mom! Dad! I-" I sat up, I was sweating everywhere. The stupid Prisoner did this, didn't he? I tried to wipe the sweat from my forehead when I realized that my arms had been tied behind my back, and my crystal was gone.

I was sitting down against a pile of rubble, I looked around and saw that a short distance away from me was The Prisoner, tending to Ashen and Valen's injuries. I tried using mind-control on him, but it was hopeless. I was in no condition to use my powers right now.

The Prisoner turned around to look at me. "Oh, you're

finally awake now!" he exclaimed. He walked over to me.

"You did that on purpose, didn't you?" I accused.

"Did what on purpose?" he asked. Although, I was pretty sure he knew exactly what I was talking about. "Oh, I know what you mean," he said. "When you were knocked out, you experienced a memory didn't you?"

I nodded. "Yes, and it wasn't a rather pleasant one."

The Prisoner looked me in the eyes. "Robyn, I- well, I think I should tell you something."

I raised my eyebrows, it seemed like he actually needed to inform me of something important.

"I thought you'd have put the pieces together after you'd experienced the memory again," he continued. "But since it seems like you haven't, I suppose I'll have to tell you."

"Well, spit it out then," I demanded.

"Well, you know how the death of your parents was caused by Aquas?"

"Of course I know that."

"The two Aquas might have been related to someone you were close to…"

"Who?"

"Nova. The child of the two Aquas was Nova."

I didn't really know what to say. It couldn't be true. Nova's parents were… murderers. Though not just any murders, but the ones who killed my parents.

"That can't be true," I wept.

"I'm afraid it is."

I looked up at The Prisoner. "Well, just because Nova's parents did that, doesn't mean Nova is like that too."

On the Other Side

"*Was* like that too," the Prisoner corrected me.

I wanted to punch him in the face for that. I didn't know what to say, I couldn't quite believe what he had told me. Nova never told me that.

He kept using mind-control to keep me on the ground. I looked over at Ashen and Valen who desperately needed medical attention. I looked back at the Prisoner.

"I can't believe this."

chapter 28
I Struggle to Make a Choice

The Prisoner left me tied up on the ground while he continued to assist Ashen and Valen with their wounds. The Prisoner was wrapping bandages around the place where Valen's wrist *used* to be. Ashen had taken his shirt off and was pressing it against the cut on his chest, doing his best to stop the bleeding.

Since I hadn't killed them, did that mean I wouldn't get Nova back? Did I even want Nova back, now that I knew she'd kept this secret from me? I did want my parents back though. Maybe if they came back, we could run away from this place and go find a new life somewhere else.

The voice still hadn't said anything to me. I didn't know what my next move would be, though I knew that first off, I needed to get my hands untied. As well as the crystal, the Prisoner had taken my dagger. He'd used thick rope to tie me with, and the knot was extremely tight. I looked around to see if there was anything sharp I could use to cut the rope with. Nothing. I was running out of ideas.

I think I can help you, said the voice.

I was wondering when you were going to show up, I replied.

I thought the voice was going to give me instructions, like usual, but it appeared I was wrong.

The ground in front of me started to glow, and I began to feel light-headed. I watched the ground grow brighter. Then, little pieces of light began forming together. It was hard to explain what I was seeing, it was almost as if these small lights were coming together to form something. I glanced over at Ashen and the other two; they didn't seem to notice what was going on. The lights kept collecting together until they formed something.

It was a... a person.

Before I could say anything to the figure, something happened. The lights all began to turn dark and slowly morphed into flesh. What was once a beautiful light figure, had now turned into a horrific-looking flesh-being. It wasn't exactly easy to describe what I was looking at, the best way was to say that it looked *horrendous.* The figure stood in front of me. It didn't have facial features but I could tell that it was looking at me.

Is this your idea of help? I asked the voice.

The figure started laughing at me. It was odd to see something that didn't have a mouth laugh.

It pointed at its chest. "Well, who do you think I am dear?"

"You're the voice that's been in my head all this time?" I exclaimed.

"That would be me!" the figure replied. I didn't think that this is what the voice would look like, but I knew the voice was on my side, so looks aside, the figure and I were a team.

I pointed at Ashen, Valen, and Zed. "How have they not noticed you already?"

"Unless you give someone permission, you are the only person who can see, hear, and feel me."

"Permission?"

"Yes, if you grant someone permission to see your guiding voice, they'll be able to see me. Otherwise, they can't see me at all."

"Why is that?" I asked.

"It's almost as if I'm a figment of your imagination, but only, I'm actually here."

"So then… not a figment of my imagination."

"No, not really."

This guy wasn't making a whole lot of sense.

"So then, what are you exactly?" I asked.

"It's kind of a long story. Just think of me as a person, just like you."

"Okay, but that still doesn't explain why I'm the only one who can see you."

The flesh figure stood in silence for a moment.

"To be honest, I'm not quite sure why that is either, I think it's that way because I have such a strong connection with the person I guide, and so whoever's head I'm in, is the person who can see me."

That was a good enough explanation for me.

"So what's the plan?" I asked.

"First, let's untie the rope." The figure began to untie the knot.

I tried not to wince as he got closer to me, it was as if a human had no skin, so all you could see were the muscles and flesh. Once the knot was undone, I already felt myself getting stronger. I felt ready to use my powers again.

"I think I should be able to use mind-control to get back the Mind Crystal, and the dagger," I told the figure.

It nodded slowly. "Are you sure you're already strong enough to use powers?" it inquired. "What happened before with the Prisoner drained a lot of your energy."

Speaking of the Prisoner, he hadn't yet noticed that my hands were untied. Neither had Ashen or Valen. I slowly stood up, trying not to make a noise. The second I was up on two feet, I began to feel light-headed and dizzy.

The figure was right, a lot of my power and energy had been drained, but I couldn't let that stop me. Usually, I preferred mind-control over emotion control, but at that moment, I thought emotion control might work.

"I think I have a plan," I told the figure. "If I control the Prisoner's emotions, and make him feel sorry for tying me up and taking my stuff, then he'll probably give me my belongings back, and I can then get away."

"The plan is good, for the most part," replied the flesh figure. "Though I do have a couple of issues with it."

I nodded, waiting for it to tell me what was wrong with my plan.

"First of all," he started, "I still don't think you're strong enough to use your powers yet." I rolled my eyes. "And second of all, when you've got the crystal and dagger, you say that we can get away. Where do you plan on going?"

I ignored the first question and moved straight to the second, the figure had a good point. Where was I going to go? Surely everyone still alive wanted me dead, right? It wasn't safe for me anymore.

"I don't know," I said finally.

"That's not a good enough answer," he responded. I knew it wasn't, but the truth was, I really didn't know what I was going to do.

"Looks like we're about to get some company," the figure said.

I looked to the right and saw the Prisoner heading my way. He didn't look like he cared that I wasn't tied up anymore. This was my chance to use my powers and put my plan into action. The only problem was that my 'plan' hadn't been fully thought-out.

"Robyn," Zed said. "I'm not going to use mind-control on you."

Well, too bad, I thought, *because I'm going to use it on you*. I focused my mind and tried to make the Prisoner give me back my crystal and dagger. Suddenly, my head began to hurt. It felt like the world's worst-ever headache.

Zed looked at me, expressionless. "Robyn, you're too weak to use your powers right now. It's going to take a little while for you to recover."

I was angry, what was I supposed to do without my powers? I didn't know what was next for me. Here I was face to face with the Prisoner and I had no idea what my next move would be.

"Robyn, you have a choice to make here. You can either be a wanted criminal, and spend your life on the run. Or you can fix your mistakes, and become good again."

I thought about it for a moment. "I can't become good again. Surely, I'll be sentenced to death because of what I've done."

"I imagine they'll just keep you in prison for a long time."

"Why would I want to be in prison? I'd rather be on the run than have to be stuck in a prison cell for the rest of my life."

"Robyn, just trust me. It's better to be locked up in prison, then have your powers consume you."

I looked at the flesh figure.

Don't listen to him, Robyn. Let's just run away. You'll have me to guide you, so nothing can go wrong.

I didn't know what to do. I wanted to run away, and start a new life, with the voice guiding me. Though something inside of me was telling me that I needed to own my mistakes and go to prison for all that I'd done.

Robyn, don't you understand that you'll have to go to prison for a very long time? Imagine how depressing it will be.

"You're right," I said aloud.

"Who's right?" asked Zed.

"Oh yeah, I forgot you can't see him."

"See who?"

"It doesn't matter." The crystal and the dagger didn't matter anymore. I just needed to get away before I was taken to prison.

On the Other Side

I looked at the figure, he gave me a nod, assuring me that he knew what I was going to do. I felt like a coward doing it, but I took one last look at Ashen and Valen, then turned away from the Prisoner, and ran.

After about 300 yards, the voice stopped me. *Aren't you forgetting something?*

"Like what?" I questioned

"You need the gem to get back your parents *and* Nova," they said.

"I thought you said we should run!"

"*After* you get the gem."

"Well what now? Go back? I can't use my powers, remember?!" I protested.

"Then I guess they'll stay dead." The fleshy figure turned to leave. I knew it was a play but I still had to stop them.

"Wait!" I yelled. "What's the plan?"

"Zed has a soft spot for you. He can relate to you. I know you're very persuasive, even without your powers."

I turned and looked back at Zed, who was watching me as I ran. I don't know why he didn't pursue me.

The voice and I jogged back to Zed and the others.

'Z-Zed, please I need the stone." I said, really trying to convey a sense of hopelessness. Perhaps he might give in if I put on enough of a show. "Please!" I begged him.

"Why?" he inquired.

"It is the only way to stop the war! It's the only way to fulfill the quest!" I lied. Or so I thought.

"No, it isn't, do you believe in yourself?"

"Yes! Trust me, it's the only thing that makes sense."

I was actually starting to believe what I said at this point. "It's 'Band together for ye need fight. So the world shant plunge into eternal night.' I know what it means!"

I looked at the voice's body, I assumed at that point that that line meant join the voice, I no longer cared about 'plunging the world into night'. I didn't know what it meant, I just needed my family back.

"I need the gem!" I did not intend on using my powers, but I assumed I did, for I felt dizzy as soon as I spoke that sentence. I must have used them because Zed pulled the crystal from his pocket and handed it to me reluctantly.

"I hope you make the right choice," Zed said. "For I know who your partner is. They were mine once." I looked back at what once was a voice in my head, and for the first time I felt what they were feeling. They felt scared, for some reason, in the presence of Zed.

"Come on, show yourself," Zed spoke past me.

I heard the voice say, *I grant you permission.*

I don't know what Zed saw, but by his expression I could tell he now saw them. He seemed unfazed by the muscle tissue spread across a once human body.

"Hello again Zed," the voice said. I was so confused. How did they know each other?

"Hand me the gem, Robyn," the voice spoke again through its non-existent mouth.

"I wouldn't do that if I were you. Do you even know their plan?" Zed said.

I turned to the voice. "It's true, why did you come to me?"

"Only to help you, Robyn."

ing. A bead of sweat trickled down my neck as I forced a beam of energy through the stone like we had done with the dragon. The voice let out a horrendous wail. It ripped free of my grasp on its mind. I had no interest in calling them *"they"* anymore. It wasn't human at all. Even if it once was.

"Zed! I'm not strong enough! Take the stone!" I yelled.

I tossed him the gem. He looked at me and nodded.

He forced another beam of power through the gem. It was so much brighter I had to avert my eyes.

Zed forced the Voice to its knees and I drew my sword.

I struck the voice in the stomach but before my sword made contact I felt a searing pain in my right shin. I sliced its arm off right at the joint. I pulled the 'flesh sword' from my leg and screamed in pain as I did so.

I was getting angry.

I sliced the voice through its chest. It hollered in agony as its muscles treaded and intertwined themselves with themselves to attempt to heal the wound. It had done this before, but not with their arm; once the limb was detached it could no longer be healed.

I looked over to Zed who was standing further back now. He was out of range from the voice so he could keep his concentration without being sliced to bits. He pushed his arms forward with some struggle and yelled: "Stop moving!"

The voice didn't. Instead he stabbed me in my abdomen. I cried out as Zed said the same thing to me as I said to him, "I'm not strong enough!"

"Together then!"

On the count of three we both yelled, "GO STILL!"

The voice stopped, it writhed and struggled against its imaginary bonds. I brought my sword down on its head.

The voice fell and disappeared in a cloud of smoke. With a hiss it evaporated with one final set of words: *These are not your friends.*

I stumbled back and sat down hard on the ground. The stone fell from Zed's hands as he did the same. He picked it back up of course. I bandaged up my wounds and kept my sword unsheathed. In case the voice came back, but it didn't seem like it would. For they may have been powerful, but they weren't immortal.

That was when I spotted the guards.

chapter 29
Origin Stories Are Always Tragic

✳✳✳

I laughed, running around the tiny swing set, chasing my little brother with a smile. He was laughing as well. We had been playing for a while now, chasing each other around the small playground and up and down the house indoors and outdoors. I grinned at him as it was his turn to chase me. I jumped over the small wooden fence and ran off to the other side of the backyard. My brother had a harder time getting over, as he was shorter.

"Walt, I'm coming!" He giggled. I smiled and got ready to run.

For a 7 year old, he could run pretty fast. He sprinted at me, his face a look of determination and I chuckled and dashed to the side. He giggled again and turned around to face me. I ran back towards the small fence. He was close on my heels when he tripped on a rock and fell to the ground. He started to cry. I turned around and rushed back to help him.

"It hurts," He sniffled through tears.

"Where does it hurt?" I asked in a comforting tone.

"On my leg and my hand," he said with his eyes starting to water, his lips quivering slightly. I pulled up his pant leg.

He had a few scrapes on his knee, and his hand was a little scratched up from the ground.

"Don't worry Adrian, we'll get you some band-aids ok? He nodded as I picked him up and walked into the house.

"Hey mom, hey dad," I waved to my parents with my one free hand. They waved back, my mom making dinner and my dad watching TV on the couch.

I lived in a small, cozy house with three floors. The top floor was a sleeping area, the main floor was for us to eat, watch TV, and play games together, and the basement was for running around and building our lego sets.

"Just in time boys! I'm almost done with dinner!" my mom said with a smile on her face.

She was a kindly woman with lovely brown eyes and raven-black hair. She was so nice, but sometimes a little over-protective. My dad was a big man with tanned skin, a shaved head and blue eyes. He also had a beard that Adrian liked to touch because it was so big. He was always nice as well, and always tried to get us into watching football with him.

My mom squealed when she saw Adrian's scratches. "Are you okay? Do you want some band-aids for your boo-boo?" Adrian nodded his head yes.

"Hey, don't worry about it mom. I got the band-aids. You can keep going with dinner," I told my mom.

She smiled and ruffled my hair gently. "My little boy is all grown up," she said, her eyes watering. I coughed, my cheeks glowing red from embarrassment. She smiled again and I walked up the stairs. I went into the washroom and washed out his "ouchies", as my mom would call it, and then grabbed a band-aid. I put two on his knee and one on his hand.

"Does it feel better now?" I asked him. He nodded slightly as mom called us for dinner.

"Kids, dinner's ready! Wash your hands and come downstairs!"

We washed our hands and we both made our way downstairs. The table was all set up with the food ready to eat. My dad was sitting at the table.

"Hey kiddos, you ok?" He grinned at us. We smiled and nodded at him. We ate our dinner, talking about the day.

Today we had a day off because of holidays, so I didn't have to go to training. Soon I'll become a full-fledged member of the Embers!

Our family have been Embers for as long as we can remember, and our great-great- great-great- great-great-great-great-grandfather was actually one of the first founders of our kingdom! My dad was the head of the Embers, and my mom worked as a teacher for the Embers.

My dad sighed as we asked him about his day. "Tensions are slowly rising between the four sectors. There have been disagreements between members of different sectors. It doesn't seem very severe right now, but it's still a problem." My mom's face fell and I slumped in my chair.

I wouldn't be able to see Aurora anytime soon then. We would have fun hanging out and catching movies together. She was the love of my life, but she was an Aqua. I don't even think she knows that I like her, I thought sadly. Adrian looked confused but didn't say anything.

My thoughts were interrupted by my dad asking me a question.

"Hey Walt, how was your day?" I looked up from my pasta and shrugged.

"It was okay, but I didn't really do much. I just played with Adrian, watched some TV, played some video games, and practiced my powers," I responded.

My dad narrowed his eyes in confusion. "Don't you have training today? It's not the weekend right?..."

The rest of the family groaned teasingly. My dad was super infamous for forgetting things. If it didn't happen at least once a day, you would be surprised.

He looked confused and asked, "What did I miss?"

"Today's a holiday daddy," Adrian said knowingly.

"Even Adrian knows the schedule for training, and he hasn't even been initiated yet!" I said with a chuckle.

We all cracked up, my dad still looking confused. We finished our dinner and decided to play a game. We had many choices but decided on Ember Monopoly. The whole board, including the properties, were fire-themed, and there were some special rules. You could only land on waterworks if you had a protection shield, otherwise you would lose a random property and 500 dollars. Tough.

There are also rules about how the red properties are more expensive than the blue ones, and how if you rolled a double, you could burn a player of your choice (100 per turn) for how many steps you rolled. There were other, more complicated rules, but it would take too long to get into them.

We were on our 6th turn and my brother was about to roll a double to get the best property in the game when the world rumbled. We looked outside and saw a *huge* tornado rolling towards us, destroying buildings and people alike. It seemed to be coming directly for us. We raced down to the basement, and huddled all together and boarded up the windows.

I went last, making sure everyone got down the stairs safely. I made sure everyone was safe, and grabbed the first aid kit just in case. Then I grabbed some food. I was cut short grabbing some snacks when I heard a blood curdling scream cut short. I raced down the stairs faster than I've ever run and saw the entire ceiling collapsed on the spot where my family used to be seconds ago.

I screamed and cried, but I needed to get out of there. Immediately.

I sprinted back up the stairs, wiping my tears off the back of my hand. The ceiling threatened to collapse as well, and I thought, *why not? I would be able to see my parents again.*

Then I saw my dad's face saying to me 'never give up' and my mom smiling at me in my mind. I sobbed as I ran out of the door, seconds before the entire house imploded and the tornado continued its destructive journey past the border mountains. I ran until I couldn't run anymore. I collapsed on a nearby hill, and cried myself to sleep.

5 YEARS LATER

I had finally found it! The spell that would bring back my family. I wiped a tear as I remembered that horrible night. I held the scroll in my hands, and skimmed past all the other powerful words and incantations for other spells. I had searched and searched for five whole years. Finally I found this scroll.

I had searched every single face of the kingdom, and I had finally found it. I had to go past the border mountains and find this Tower and this kindly old wizard had brought me up to the top of his tower, and I had asked for his scroll.

He agreed, but had placed a spell upon it so it would return to his chest after sunset. He had also given me a cryptic warning that I don't remember. It was 5:43 pm. I started the chant after drawing the proper symbols and circles on the floor and spoke every powerful word.

I channeled the grief and hopelessness I felt that night. It took a while (man that spell is long) but I (finally) got to the last stanza of the spell. It read:

The cost is far too great,
for that it is too late.
The last world spoken will,
bring the loved ones you have chosen.
Returned to your life,
And then hope it does not cause you strife.

I spoke the last word and the circle glowed. I shook faster and faster until my body was actually lifted off the ground. I spoke the names of the loved ones I had lost and as the last syllable of my brother's name slipped through my lips, I fell to the ground, quivering. I closed my eyes and tried to regain my energy.

It would be really awesome to fall asleep right now, I thought. I felt tired. Really tired, like I hadn't eaten anything today and hadn't gotten enough sleep. This tiredness felt like it was seeping into my bones, almost as if it was spreading through my body. But that couldn't happen right?

I opened my eyes tiredly to see my family standing in front of me, looking down at me with a surprised and shocked face. But there was something wrong. It looked like they were slightly translucent. Almost as if they were- oh no. I had brought them back as ghosts!

"Who are you, young man?" My dad's voice reached me through a long dark tunnel.

They... don't remember me, was my final thought before the world fell dark.

20 YEARS LATER

I woke up floating in the sky. I looked around, completely in confusion. The last thing I remember was my parents and brother returning as ghosts but... not remembering who I was. That probably was worse than losing them in the first place. I had brought them back to live again, but they wouldn't even know that I existed. I gritted my teeth in rage as tears slid down my face, creating silvery streaks down my cheeks.

Wait.

How was I floating?! I looked down at myself and saw... nothing. I blinked and rubbed my eyes- I didn't have hands. Or legs. Or a body. I probably didn't even have a head. I guess I'm an invisible voice floating above the ground.

Then a thought hit me. That stupid wizard! I should've paid more attention to that dumb cryptic warning. He probably said "Don't do this! You'll become a stupid flying invisible voice!" UGH! I decided then and there that I would do everything in my power to get my family back. And not like those ghost things, like real flesh and blood. I would do anything.

I looked past the horizon and past the tall border mountains and spotted the huge tower. I felt my vision go red with rage as I shot towards it. I passed through the measly gate and entered the wizard's brain. I yelled with every ounce of my being.

"TELL ME HOW TO BRING BACK MY PARENTS. OR ELSE!"

The wizard looked confused and then seemed to recognize my voice. He smiled sadly and transmitted, "I'm sorry. But there's nothing we can do. Once a spell from the Scroll of Power is spoken, nothing can be done to reverse the consequences. I already warned you."

I let free a guttural yell that made the wizard cover his ears. I growled again and left the old wizard's mind. I grieved and cried and sobbed and yelled and hurt myself but nothing would fill the empty pit inside me that was slowly growing. Yearning for revenge. In that very moment, something broke inside me like a piece of glass. I decided that if everyone that I ever loved, everyone that ever loved me were gone, then everyone else would be destroyed. Their lives would be ruined like mine. The piece of shattered glass inside me hardened and I knew I would have to take revenge or it would consume me.

I looked around and my eyes caught on a group of five teenagers looking for a magical pass through the mountains. I floated down to get a better look at them. It was like I could see through them. There was one of every element, Water, Fire, Air, Earth.

Wait. There was one more person. He seemed to be explaining something to the group. They also had some sort of special power that I hadn't ever seen before. He definitely seemed powerful.

I instantly decided that I would join this person and influence him into evil. The group successfully opened the pass and made it through, into the border mountains. They stopped to take a short break. I entered the young man's mind. What was the point of living when there was no one to live for?

What was the man's name? Let me see. It was Zed.

chapter 30
I Count Bricks

I did the first thing that came to my mind. I ran.

You might think that I'm a coward, that I was scared of what would happen to me. And that wasn't far off from the truth.

Everyone is scared of something. And even I was, despite what I thought.

I ran from everyone, I wanted out. Just to be left alone. But being who I was, that wish was very hard. Everyone knew me now. I was the mind freak who murdered people, the person who practically erased sector three from existence. I wasn't the kid who was raised in a family of Embers, the kid who had been given a quest, the kid who despite all their flaws made a couple friends.

And it hurt a bit.

I wasn't the little kid anymore.

I was the villain.

And I knew it. I knew that I'd made terrible decisions,

and kept making them. I chose wrong all the time. I enjoyed making people suffer. I enjoyed torturing my friend. And it was all because of my stupid, stupid powers. If only I had had fire powers like my parents. Everything would've been different. But I couldn't change the past. I could only make the future. My future.

I was wearing a deep red cloak. A lot of people wore cloaks of their sector's colors. So I wore red hoping that people would think I was an Ember and not well... me. It was my disguise.

And it was not working.

How could guards see me? Whenever literally anyone else wanted to be mysterious by wearing a cloak, they would stay mysterious. I was out for less than ten minutes looking like this, and I was caught.

I huffed and started to run away. But like I said before, physical activity wasn't a super strong point of mine. I quickly lost my breath and guards caught up to me.

Their uniforms looked different. They weren't red like normal. They were white. And they wore some special thing on their heads.

I tried using my powers to go free, but it wasn't working. LET ME GO.

I struggled in their arms. But they kept their firm grip on me. As I tried and tried and tried to control their minds, it wasn't working.

Then I realised their uniforms were newer. They were probably made to stop my abilities.

"Your uniforms block my powers, don't they?" I asked the guards, who were still holding on to me for dear life.

I looked from one guard to another. And they both nodded at the same time. I sighed and rolled my eyes.

I'd given up on trying to free myself, I was pretty useless without my powers.

They dragged me to the prison. I recognised the path to the high security cells and was soon thrown in one.

It was Zed's.

It had thick, gray brick walls, and a black ceiling. There were cobwebs in the corners and a small wooden stool. On the left wall there was a small bed made of metal. A sink and small toilet also accompanied the room. I looked through the bars, but as I went to touch them I was electrified. I stumbled onto the ground and just lay there, not wanting to move. I eventually fell into darkness.

※※※

It had been about a day that I'd been stuck in a cell. It was terrible. It smelled bad. The food was bad. I was lonely. Surprisingly. Normally, I would be ravished by the thought of being alone, but not now.

I guess, after being with a bunch of other people for a while, you got used to their company. But they were gone.

Nova was dead.

Rune probably hated me.

Ashen and Valen were who knows where, doing who knows what.

And I was locked in a cell.

My life was amazing.

※※※

My second day was quite like the first. Only now I was a mess. My dirty blonde hair was now knotted and I had bags under my eyes. My clothes were filthy and filled with grime (thanks to the state of my room). I counted the number of bricks that made up the walls to keep myself somewhat entertained.

Seventy-three, seventy-four, seventy-five...

Up until I reached the end.

Two hundred and twenty-five, two hundred and twenty-six, two hundred and twenty-seven.

I huffed. The small little window I had showed a storm going on outside. I heard the thunder and saw the lighting as if I were right beside it.

I bet Nova liked the rain.

I missed Nova so much.

Nova.

※※※

I woke up from my slumber by a loud crashing noise. I looked up and saw Scribe Fallon.

"How dare you interrupt my beauty sleep?" I said. "You know I need it to look this good." I pointed to myself and closed my eyes, hoping that she would just leave me alone.

"Unfortunately, I cannot do that Robyn. Come, you have a trial waiting for you." And the guards took me out of bed.

Chapter 31
The Council Decides My Fate

The Council gathered around a table in the Scribe Tower. They waited, in tense silence, for Robyn to be led into the room by the guards. All eyes were on them.

Then, Robyn was seated at a small wooden table, facing the councillors. They all wore the special white hats from the day before, in an effort to keep the witch out of their heads. The room shifted and settled as the sector heads took in this villain, who had killed so many people.

They were only a teenager.

Clearing his throat, Councillor Zephyr of the Embers took charge of the meeting.

"Today, we come together to decide the fate of Robyn Audo," he announced. "Robyn Audo is accused of killing seven hundred and eighty-three Terras and fifteen Auras," Councillor Zephyr continued.

"Robyn must pay for their crimes against the sectors!" Councilor Gaia interjected.

"I agree! Robyn cannot be allowed to walk free!" Councilor Vulcan chimed in.

"ORDER! ORDER IN THE COUNCIL!" Councillor Zephyr yelled.

"Last time we let Robyn roam free, knowing the destruction they were capable of wreaking. We cannot make the same mistake we made before. We cannot let Robyn roam free!" Councillor Gaia interjected.

"Don't free Robyn! Don't free Robyn!" Councillor Vulcan chanted.

"I SAID ORDER! ORDER IN THE COUNCIL!" Councillor Zephyr yelled.

Councillors Vulcan and Gaia stopped talking. They looked at each other, not daring to upset Councillor Zephyr again. They couldn't look at the witch seated in front of them. No matter what happened, Robyn always seemed to get the best of the Councilors.

"We need a plan. Councillor Marina, what do you think?" Councillor Zephyr asked.

"Last time, I said that Robyn is not a child and that they needed to face justice for their crimes. My decision remains the same. Serious action still needs to-" Councillor Marina started.

"Life in prison!" Councilor Gaia interjected.

"Life in prison!" Councilor Vulcan echoed.

"We will not get anywhere if you keep interrupting Councillor Gaia," Councillor Zephyr said.

Councillor Gaia looked defensively towards Councillor Vulcan who had also interrupted Councillor Marina.

"Settle down. Councillor Vulcan, any thoughts on the

matter?" Councillor Zephyr asked.

"I say life in prison! Robyn is a threat to all sectors. Let them out again and they will kill us all! Robyn killed fifteen Auras. STOP THIS NOW!" Councillor Vulcan said.

"Councillor Gaia?" Councillor Zephyr asked.

"Finally. This should be unanimous. Robyn killed over five hundred of my people. Innocent people," Councillor Gaia said, her voice quivering. "Robyn needs to spend the rest of their life in prison."

"I agree. It is settled. An unanimous vote from the five Councilors finds Robyn Audo guilty. Robyn Audo is sentenced to life in prison," Councilor Zephyr said. "Robyn Audo, you prepared a statement for the council?"

❅❅❅

Outside the Scribe tower, Ashen, Valen, and Rune walked along the street. A few minutes passed before anyone said anything. Nobody knew where to start.

"I wish I had done more to stop Robyn," Valen said at last.

"I know. If only I knocked Robyn off the dragon sooner," Ashen replied.

"It's not your fault. It's mine. If only I told Robyn the truth fast enough," Rune said.

"What do you mean?" Valen and Ashen asked simultaneously.

"You know... the reason I put Nova into the Earth," Rune replied.

Both Valen and Ashen stared back at Rune, awaiting answers.

"I - I put Nova into the Earth because I thought she was the traitor. In that moment, I was so sure it was true," Rune said.

"Wait what?" Ashen said.

"You killed Nova because you thought she was the traitor? That's ridiculous!" Valen replied.

"I thought I was trying to save us all!" Rune said defensively.

"I guess things didn't go according to plan," Valen said sarcastically.

Rune walked over to Valen and slapped him across the face. "I told you! It wasn't my fault. I tried to save us all!"

Valen held up his hands and backed up. Ashen and Valen exchanged surprised looks from the sudden turn in Rune's attitude.

"Okay, okay, we believe you. But, killing is not the answer," Valen said.

"I agree. If you think someone is going to betray us, you don't just kill them," Ashen agreed.

"I just didn't know what to do," Rune said. "It was like someone was- was in my head, urging me to do it, telling me it was the right thing to do."

"That's why we were a team," Valen said.

"Were a team?" Rune asked, confused.

Valen and Ashen did not need to respond. Rune understood what Valen meant. Valen and Ashen walked away leaving Rune alone in front of the looming Scribe tower.

chapter 32
I Leave, Goodbye!

Why did I have to pay for my decisions if I didn't regret them? Yes I killed people, I hurt people. I had good reasons. Nobody seemed to be able to grasp my perspective. I was broken and bruised. Though all people saw was how I hurt people, nobody cared if I was hurt too, if I'd lost everything. Nobody cared if my reasoning for my actions was because of that. Nobody cared about the fact that Nova was dead, she had lost everything too. Her parents, her friends, she lost Valen, Ashen, and Rune's trust. She lost her life. And now I had to live with that, which is honestly worse.

I thought about all of this as I sat in my cell, one I was used to being on the outside of. I was familiar with the surroundings, stone, darkness, iron bars, and more stone. I stayed in my cell because even when I knew I could get out, I couldn't escape myself. I wanted to see if I could live without Nova. I needed time to recuperate. Prepare. And plan.

One day the Prisoner- well, I guess he wasn't one anymore. Zed, the man I had spent many days learning from, listening to lectures on our power, just outside these bars, now stood on the other side. I had heard his footsteps along the dark corridor as he illuminated his path by lighting the torches. I flashed back to myself, remembering what had happened, what seemed like years ago.

I've been waiting for you Robyn.

The first thing he ever said to me.

As the prisoner approached my cell, I spoke.

"I've been waiting for you Zed."

He let out a small laugh, the sound reverberating off the rock. "Long staircase, isn't it?" I continued. Remembering how I followed Scribe Fallon here after my initiation, remembering how clueless and confused I'd been. Not much had changed, I still felt that way. Though the causations *had* changed. Drastically.

"Do you know why I'm here?" Zed asked.

"Do you?"

"Why wouldn't I?"

"No, I mean, do you know why I'm here? Behind these bars."

Zed looked at me with sad eyes, but did not apologize. He peered past me at the mess I had created. I suppose in the hubbub I may have thrown a tantrum and broke some things…

"Yeah," I said as I looked behind me at the tornado aftermath.

"If I could bring her back, I would." Zed spoke with certainty, he wasn't looking for reconciliation. He was above that, and I respected it.

"I'm glad society accepts you now," I said. Though I wasn't really in the mood to talk.

"I mean no one knows about my relationship in the starting of the war. They had to let me free, for there's only one cell quite like this. You know, with that key I gave you... Well, I suppose you don't have it anymore..." I did, but I didn't show. "I could've gotten out anytime I wanted, I just saw no point. This cell was my home, it wasn't a prison, it was a choice." That answered my questions on why he didn't just, you know *make* me set him free.

"So you mean you just stayed here?" I questioned.

"Yes, though one day I thought, if I traveled beyond the border mountains I could see what was unknown. I suppose you know, don't you?"

"How could I forget-" my voice broke. Beyond the mountains was a grassy field, oak trees and a beautiful memory. Even if her parents hurt mine, my fondness of Nova, and the moment we shared under the largest tree in the unending rolling hills, would stay unsullied by anything until the end of time.

Oh Nova, I miss you. I thought to myself. My parents, I loved them of course, but it was so long ago. I would remember them forever. The image of my mother and father's faces were becoming blurry. The fact that one day I might forget what they looked like, sounded like, brought tears to my eyes. But I wouldn't forget *them,* who they were to me and the ones who loved them.

I remembered the way Nova talked about her family, how she always looked guilty. She shouldn't have. I wouldn't have blamed the person I loved for something they did not do. How I wished she'd told me so she could've let go of that guilt. She wasn't ready. She and I needed more closure before either of us could let go. Sadly, it was a little too late. There was no moving on now.

A single tear drop slid down my cheek. Zed watched me as it trailed down my face and landed in my palm. I enclosed it in my fingers.

"Can I continue?" The ex-Prisoner said. I had forgotten what we were talking about. I was so lost in memories.

"I'll take your silence as a yes, then," he continued. "One day while I was pondering my plan to leave, to see if I could indeed escape, the prophet arrived."

"Prophet? You mean you had a quest too?"

"No, well yes, see before I was locked up I too had a quest to fulfill."

"But how?"

"I'm a lot older than you think."

Wow, I thought to myself, *you must be, like 400!*

He smiled as if reading my thoughts. "Well, I'm not that old, don't worry." He continued. "My quest was similar to yours, there was a voice in my head urging me on. I suppose I failed. I thought the voice was a hoax, a force with no solid form. Until you came along, that is. The voice abandoned me, once it realized I wasn't the one. They had a plan to control everyone's mind like it did yours. Rule the world in secrecy."

I could just hear them saying that: *rule the world in secrecy.* Not a bad idea. I quickly shoved that aside so I could listen, but that did sound intriguing.

"I hadn't been through enough. The voice didn't have anything to grasp on to, to fuel me. So they drove me insane. I plunged the world into war once before this, you know. Then I ended up here," he gestured at my cell.

"When the Prophet arrived in the flesh I was worried. Anyone would be. They said... hmm, I can't remember exactly but not long after I was sentenced to prison for life, she told me-" I cut him off.

"Is this still the same Prophet?" I asked.

"There has only ever been *one* prophet. Other than the one who was banished. Untrustworthy was the wizard in the mountains. Crazy old man, but I guess that's not his fault. He was supposed to be a prophet but couldn't handle the pressure."

"So you mean he was crazy *before* he drank all that tea?" I said with mild sarcasm.

"Haha, yes. After the removal of his powers went, um sideways, he went a little mad. He still can see glimpses of the future, along with other... odd things. The Prophet is reborn every 500 years. We're all really quite oblivious to the ways of the prophet."

"No kidding," I said under my breath.

"She told me about a young child, not man nor woman. *Elusive is the red chested bird,* I believe she said. The robin. She spoke of great powers, and for a new prophecy to be issued when the time was right. Boy was that a long time for it to be right. After that she disappeared. She spoke her last words before she disappeared into smoke, not to be seen by *anyone* until you. She told me to help you, to make sure you were on the right path..." he paused and sighed. "I guess I didn't. Or maybe we both just needed to learn."

Learn what? He was so vague sometimes it frustrated me almost more than Valen used to.

"I won't bear witness to your escape. Nor will I inform them how you did it. Consider your secrets safe with me." Then he left.

❖❖❖

That night, I felt around my pockets as I lay in my 'bed', if you could call it that. A mattress pressed to the side of the room and one crusty pillow filled with goose hair. Nova would've told me that they were feathers, so I called it hair. Even in death we could still fight.

I found my key, a flat stone piece with an emblem engraved on it. I tossed it up and catched a few times, debating if I should or shouldn't stay. I realized then that even though the voice was evil, it could still be right. It could still guide me, for it hadn't done me much wrong, until it tried to kill me. If they weren't hellbent on ruling, would things have been different? If I sided with the voice, how would things be for me now? Would Nova be back in my arms? Did I make the right choice? I must have. Cause what would've been a better outcome than this?

I drifted off to sleep thinking about Nova, how much I missed her, and the voice. It's silky yet rough tone, echoing off the wall in my mind as it spoke. Commanding but gentle. It was right, Nova wasn't my friend. She was my everything.

On the Other Side

I heard what the prisoner had said over and over in my dreams. *They had a plan to control everyone's mind like it did yours. Rule the world in secrecy.* I knew then what I would do. I wouldn't control everyone, and I might not have been good at secrets but I could rule. And once again, the voice told me how.

❖❖❖

I awoke in the morning? There were no windows. For all I knew 8 years had passed and time was in reverse.

I fumbled around in my jean pocket for my magic wall bending stone. The stone didn't open the iron bars though. Luckly, it didn't have to.

"You sly little…" I trailed off and shook my head. Zed had unlocked my cell door before he left. I could've picked the lock you know. I stepped outside the cell for the first time in… months? Jeez, what was time anymore?

I walked to the end of the hallway and to the large iron door. I unlocked it like I had many times before when I came here for training. I set the stone ablaze and lit a torch like the scribe had done. I walked through the narrow pathway, up the circular staircase and opened the stone wall that led into a musty old alleyway.

As soon as I stepped into the sun I was blinded. It was early. Like 5 A.M, early. I didn't like early.

I got a passing person to go buy me a change of clothes. I made sure he would tell no one he saw me when he got back. You decide what that meant. I put on the black cargo pants, white short sleeve top and my flannel button-up I asked him to get from home.

I snuck around town, no doubt looking sketchy to the odd person that saw me. Don't worry, they didn't recognise me because I told them not to.

Once I got out of the busy part of town I called my dragon.

Thankfully, he came.

I was so glad to see him. I got astride him and left for the end of the world.

That's just what we magics call the edge of the magical kingdom. I flew in and out of the clouds, enjoying our last ride together.

We spotted the non-magic kingdom from above. Their old Victorian houses and subjugation by class was saddening. Did I really want to live there? I looked back at my old home, the rounded glass buildings of the Aqua's territory being rebuilt. The green magic glowed from the Terra's territory as they put back their land bit by bit, most likely building log cabins to go there later.

I thought fondly of how I made Rune do, and watch most of that. God I hated her. I saw the weird hyper-modern houses of the Aura division. And finally the tall Edwardian style homes in the Ember division, my old home. Of course, all sectors were color-coded, my parents' and my old house painted a medium red.

Well, even though it *was* beautiful, I hated it. I knew that I couldn't live there; I didn't want solitude past the border mountains, nor did I want to alter the memory of Nova and I. I didn't want to live with a crazy old ex-prophet wizard who had magic scrolls that confused me. So I landed outside the gates.

I patted my dragon on the snout. I pressed my head to his, the coldness of his scales chilling me. I stayed there a moment before telling him to go back to the others. To live in peace until I ever called on him. I told him to uphold his duty, for while the other dragons fought for their elemental tribe, he was supposed to stop them.

"Keep the worlds at peace while I'm gone, will ya?" I said to him. Then I whispered a melancholy "I love you."

The dragon bowed to me and took off into the sky. The end of the summer sun shining and reflecting off his glassy wings. Through the transparency of the webbing, like a prism, light refracted and created the most gorgeous and only rainbow shower I had ever seen.

I turned towards the gate and stepped through.

chapter 33
My Turn

I'd never crossed the border between the magic and no magic side before. Of course I'd heard stories about no-magics but that was about it. In reality, very few Magic people had ever crossed the border. People that didn't have magic weren't allowed to cross. They would probably mess up our magic somehow.

This place was somewhat similar to my world. There were many houses, roads, and buildings. The main difference was that they had one ruler. Who would agree on having just one ruler? They would have way too much power, being the only one in charge. *I* wanted to be the only one in charge and *I* wanted 'too much' power.

You know how if I wanted something, I would take it?

I walked in the middle of the road with no problems until I got to an intersection. *STOP!* I calmly screamed in my head. The cars stopped so I could keep walking. People stared at me but I didn't care. They wished they could be as cool as me.

While the no magics did know about our elemental powers, they had no idea about my special powers. That meant they would never see me coming. I maniacally laughed in my head.

I walked over to some lady selling things and asked, "Where is the castle? Where is the King?"

"O-over th-there." She was very shaky and old. Whatever, I had more important things to do than help some old lady.

After about a ten minute walk, I got to the castle. It was very grand and beautiful. Nova would've loved it I bet. The castle was very ancient and classical compared to the rest of the modern city.

Time for a little fun, I thought, as I cracked my knuckles and tilted my head.

I walked up the grand staircase, trailing my fingers along the wall next to it. I finally reached the top and I was out of breath but the two guards couldn't know that, for it might be seen as a sign of weakness. And *I* was not weak.

"Excuse me... uh, what is your name?" The guard was the nervous one here.

"Robyn. My name is Robyn."

"Yes, well excuse me Robyn, you can't be here right now unless you are faculty or royalty." He stood up tall.

"Oh, well actually," I stood taller. "I can."

Let me through, I thought, very clearly.

The weak little guard stood aside and let me through.

I pushed open the ginormous doors and marched through them, not bothering to close them.

The ceiling was very tall. On it were many old paintings. That could be changed when I started ruling this place. The architecture was very old, but very cool. *I think I'll keep those.* I walked through the rest of the castle listing any changes I would want to make when this was all mine.

"Excuse me, but who are you?" One of the servants. No, one of *my* servants.

"Note to self, when I rule I will get servants that don't ask so many questions."

"What do you mean when you rule? We have a ruler and you won't be-"

Just stop talking. I got annoyed. Why couldn't everyone just know how amazing of a ruler I would be?

Done with the first floor improvement list, I was now going up.

At the top of the staircase there was a beautiful big fountain. I felt a tear swell up in my eye. *Nova would love that.* I quickly wiped it away.

I found the king in his office. There were two guards positioned outside but I quickly gained access to the room by telling them there was a huge fire in the kitchen. Now, I knew I could just use my powers, (that was plan B), but nothing compared to the fear on their faces when I said there was a fire. Then, when I thought about it, I wished I actually had lit a fire. That would've been fun.

I pushed open the door.

"Don't you remember our conversation about knocking,

Mason?" the king said, without looking up from his computer.

"Oh, it's not Mason. I'm Robyn, the newest monarch."

The king looked very scared.

"Oh sorry, Carter but it's been decided." No one ever called the king 'Carter'. They called him, Your Majesty, King or King Carter, but recently, he had lost his crown. To me.

"No, no, I am the king. How- how did you get in here?" He hid behind his chair. As if that would protect him.

"You'll find I can be very," how do I put it? "Persuasive." I smiled.

"Guards! Guards!" he yelled.

"Oh they're not here. They are busy putting out a fire." I made air quotes with my hands when I said fire.

I confidently walked towards the desk. As I walked towards it, Carter walked away from it. I sat down in his chair and spun around a few times before he said, "No, get off. That's top grain leather."

"Great," I replied. "Only the best for me." I swiped everything off of the marble and glass table and then put my feet up on it.

"Oh no not my table too!"

I was going to have to start using my powers soon.

Make me the official ruler, I commanded Carter.

He read out of a very formal book and made me monarch of the no-magics.

"Now, let me speak to the people!" I commanded.

"What?! No, I will never!"

Oh, I forgot. *Let me speak to the people,* I thought again.

He brought me a screen that would showcase to everyone.

"Hello, people of whatever! I am the new ruler and you *will* obey me!"

People booing me? I didn't care. *I* was in control now.

"I hope you all respect my authority, otherwise... I will make you obey me."

Carter stood up and tried to walk out.

"Uh-uh," I snapped. "Come back here." He came back. "Actually, no. Go get me... something." Carter walked out.

He came back with a fancy cheese platter.

"I did not ask for that!" I walked over to him, grabbed the platter, and dumped it onto his half bald head. I pushed the doors open and walked to the front of the castle.

Ignoring the guards, I headed down the front stairs. I turned to look at the castle. *This is all mine now.* I smiled very wide and stood up tall.

Epilogue

10 YEARS LATER

Robyn tapped a finger against the armrest of the throne on which they sat.

As the clock struck noon and the church bells rang out in the distance, they rose and paced around the throne room, awaiting Charles for the sixth time that day.

As if on cue, a stout man in a top hat burst through the door, sweating and red-faced. Robyn's eyes shifted to the grandfather clock collecting dust in the corner. "You're late," they said, examining their fingernails.

"My apologies, your majesty. Now, shall we get started?" Charles stammered.

Robyn took a seat upon their throne once again. "Show me."

Charles pulled a small bag from his coat pocket. "H-here they are, your majesty."

He handed the bag to Robyn. They opened it and peered inside, examining the precious gems inside.

"Emeralds, sapphires, rubies, diamonds, garnets, and

opals. All you asked for," Charles said, removing his hat and running his fingers along the brim.

Robyn frowned. "My, my. Forgetful, aren't we? Do you not remember that I explicitly asked for topaz this time? You know how I love them," they chided.

"S-sorry your majesty."

Robyn snapped. At their command, Charles placed a hand on his head, one at the base of his chin, and sharply jerked his head to the side. With a nauseating crack, Charles crumpled to the ground. Robyn seemed unfazed, dumping the gems into their hands.

"I'm sorry too, Charles."

❖❖❖

"Let the tournament commence!" announced Emmie.

Her proclamation was met with cheers and chants from her fellow players, Leo, James, and Skylar.

"I'm thinking of a number between one and ten," Emmie said, tucking a golden curl behind her ear and pushing her glasses up a little farther on her nose.

"Five!" James shouted.

"Nuh uh. Try again!" Emmie exclaimed.

"Two?" Leo suggested.

"Wrong again!" Emmie told him.

"Seven!" Skylar said. Emmie nodded. "Ding ding ding!"

Leo and James groaned.

Skylar shuffled her deck with closed eyes. She yanked free a card and slapped it on the table. On the card was an image of a woman with angular features and stark-white hair, wielding a lethally sharp icicle. "Ezra, The Snow Queen! Five-hundred damage," Skylar, a dark-skinned girl with colourful beads in her braids boasted.

Leo, a chubby red-haired boy, scoffed. He shuffled his deck and pulled a card, placing it on the table. Plastered on the card's front was a scaly woman, who seemed to be half octopus from the waist down. "Mesia, The Sea Witch! Eight-hundred damage!" Leo bellowed.

"Oh crap!" Skylar said, the slightest twinge of admiration in her tone.

Emmie shuffled. With an exhale, she pulled a card from her deck. She grinned as she threw it down. On the card was an alarmingly thin man in black. "Jordy, the Shadow! One-thousand damage!"

Leo slapped his hands over his mouth. Skylar let out an audible gasp.

"That's nothing," James said. He shuffled his deck and slowly pulled out a card, gently placing it beside Emmie's.

Emmie wiped the lenses of her spectacles on her shirt sleeve to make sure what she was seeing was true. Skylar let out an even louder gasp, and Leo simply stood and flipped the chair he'd been sitting on.

The villain could have only been about sixteen years of age, with curls of honey blonde hair and a lethally evil grin on their face. The villain rode atop a crystal dragon.

James laced his fingers. "Robyn, the Witch. Three thousand damage."

※※※

Myth and Magic Crew 10

I like to think of myself as a strong person. I've proven not only to others, but to myself, that I can handle anything. The loss of my parents broke me, and yet, here I am. I got through that on my own. I didn't turn to alcohol, I didn't consider suicide. If that couldn't push me over the edge, why would this be able to? These were my thoughts going into the quest. And yet, the sheer thought of it wakes me up in a cold sweat every night. I can no longer sleep a second without seeing battles raging, people dying at my own hand. And I see her. I see my love, the only person in this whole damn world who made me feel like a person, dead. That pushed me over the edge. That turned me into what you see before you today. Kill me. Seeing her, remembering the sound of her laugh every single day of my life knowing I will never get her back, is a fate worse than death. For the first time in my life, I sympathize with those who scream to burn the witch.

–Spoken by the perpetrator, at the trial of Robyn Audo.

About the Authors

Aafreen Jessani is a 13 year old eighth grader who lives in Mississauga, Ontario. She enjoys reading and writing fantasy novels. Some of her favourite stories are The Land of Stories, Harry Potter and Keeper of Lost Cities. In her free time, she has written mystery filled books by herself and with friends. She would like to thank her fellow peers and writers for their amazing ideas and constant support that made this story.

Charlotte L.H Hansen is a 14 year old 9th grader who lives in Toronto ON. She loves art, as well as writing and reading. She has written unpublished books for herself, on her own or with friends. This is her first official public book. She would Like to thank her fellow writers for their fantastic ideas and support.

Marcus Lau is a 12 year old 7th grader who lives in Toronto, Ontario. He enjoys reading and writing fanfiction as well as new unpublished books. He also likes to practice Taekwondo regularly. This is his first official published book. He would like to thank his friends, family, and fellow writers for their incredible writing styles and ideas, as well as their unrelenting support, even through late-night writing sessions.

Mischa Wijesekera is a 14 year old 9th grader who lives in Houston, Texas. She enjoys reading, writing, and debating as well as playing competitive tennis, skiing, and travelling around the world. She would like to thank her mother, father, and older brother, Mikail, for their constant support and encouragement. She looks forward to publishing another book in the near future!

Saffron Gibson is fourteen year old 9th grader who lives in Toronto, Ontario with her parents, and two younger siblings. She enjoys reading and writing stories, as well as listening to music and spending time with her friends. She would like to thank her friends and family for their support, and our story director Emily for making this book possible :)

Siena Chiaradia is a thirteen-year-old eighth grader who currently resides in Toronto, Ontario with her mother, father, and younger brother. She enjoys reading stories as well as writing her own, and sharing them with others. She would like to thank absolutely no one, as she did everything herself. <3

Sophia Alfano is a thirteen year old eighth grader who lives and was raised in Harrison, New York. She enjoys playing softball, writing, and playing video games. This is her first published book, but hopefully it won't be her last.

Veronica Pare is a 13 year old eight grader who lives in North Glengarry, Ontario. She loves reading, theatre, art, Harry Potter and spending time with her friends. She would like to thank her parents and her friend, who have supported her.